"*Two souls in o*
Will never be a
Two girls in one life,
With a path full of limits and needs.
Two stories to tell,
Full of notes which will never be read.
Two pieces of puzzle,
With edges not meant to connect."

Two Souls in One Body

Alinar Den

Published by ALINAR, 2023.

TWO SOULS IN ONE BODY

First edition. August 28, 2023.

ISBN: 979-8223039358

Written by Alinar Den.

Beth

Street noise, cool air, warm blanket...

3...2...1

Beth opened her eyes. Eyelids so heavy. Sunlight streaming through the window, almost blinding. She closed her eyes again.

3...2...1

She covered her face with a blanket and opened her eyes again. Small green square pattern was blurry. She touched the cloth with her fingertips just to feel its texture, rough but warm. Slowly Beth pulled her face from under the blanket.

"OK..." she said to herself. "Only a bit blurry, but I'm back. Maybe we just need new curtains, so it will not be that painful... I wonder..."

Beth put on her glasses and took the notebook and pen from a nightstand.

"We should think of it together... color of the curtains. Maybe something dark, to kill the light completely..."

She opened the notebook to write it down, but stopped seeing the message in a funky handwriting. Letters were going up and down, without following any lines. One was smaller than another. This handwriting was a mess, but Beth smiled when she saw it.

"How can you write this way?"

For a second Beth thought that it was surprisingly not frustrating. This was the only mess that she found cute. Normally messy people bugged her. Beth was always trying to fix them, make them neater or help them be more organized. But not this one. She couldn't help it, she stopped trying many years ago. Any was the biggest mess ever, but Beth just couldn't change it. Irony... but now it felt cute, even this horrible handwriting that looked like it was written by a child trying to hold an uncontrollably moving pen.

Beth touched the page of the notebook. Glossy page was rougher than normal. Any's palms were sweating while she was writing it.

"Interesting..."

Before reading Beth looked around the room. Everything was in place. She could see how hard Any was trying to please her by returning things back where they belonged, the way Beth liked it.

"Or years of training finally worked... or she really wants something from me."

Beth decided not to delay it any longer and started reading:

"Hi Beth,

Thank you so much for this day! I really enjoyed it. I accidentally opened Karl's message. He said that the deal with North Wing is a success. He said you're a genius and that he will never argue with you again. It took him time to realize it though..."

Any drew a smiley face after those words. She couldn't hide the irony. It took her much longer to realize that Beth is always right. Beth smiled again. She enjoyed being right, but she loved when people admitted that. Any knew what to start the conversation with to please her. Now Beth wondered even more what Any wanted from her and continued reading:

"Anyway. No more phone calls or messages. On the way out I met Trev from 202 and he complimented my scarf. He said that it highlights my eyes. Guys... He didn't realize I was wearing lenses, not glasses, that's why my eyes looked different."

Any drew a smiley face again, just to confirm how amusing she found Trev.

"Not like our eyes are not beautiful behind glasses. Well, you know what I mean. By the way, can you check if I put lenses in the liquid. I hope I didn't leave them out like last time."

Beth stopped reading and pulled out the drawer of the night stand.

Lenses were in a container. Beth nodded with appreciation and continued reading:

"I know you're busy at work lately, but can I have one more day next week? It is so beautiful outside and I just wanted to go to this park during fall... it's a bit far, but I want it so badly. I took some pictures for you today..."

Beth flipped the notebook page and saw a few Polaroid photos attached to it.

Forest, lake, yellow leaves. Smiley face framed by messy ginger hair and that tacky orange scarf. Any knitted it herself and was so proud of it. It was straight after she knotted Beth that socks . Beth was wearing them at home because they were not fitting in any of her shoes.

Beth looked at Any's face again. Her eyes did look different without glasses. She could clearly see it even in the photo. Dark brown with a crack of orange and yellow, like a lava streaming down the volcano.

Beth pulled the small mirror from the nightstand and looked at herself. Her hair looked like she was riding a motorcycle without a helmet. Beth took her glasses off and looked into the mirror again. She barely could see the yellow cracks in her brown eyes now. Beth put her glasses on again and looked at the Polaroid picture once again. Any was smiling like someone asked her to show all her teeth. Her eyes were glowing. Beth looked at the mirror again. She never smiled that way, even for a photo. She barely showed her teeth while smiling, considering them too big and ugly.

Beth removed Any's photo from the notebook page and wrote with neat cursive "Any, Sep 23". Holding a photo in her hand she slid out of bed, opened a walk-in closet and pulled out a big board with a lot of photos attached to it.

Beth touched the corner of a photo with a huge "Welcome home" banner behind a big group of people. Small arrows were drawn between faces and handwritten messages. Beth found a smiley face of her neighbor Trev. He was tall and very thin, with long curly hair, wearing a bunch of horribly mismatched colorful clothes. His message said: "Trev, apt 202. Single. Has a yellow Labrador called Lucy. Adorable!"

Beth mumbled: "Is he adorable or the dog?". She added to a note:

"Likes an orange scarf."

Beth looked at the photo again and pointed her finger at Any standing two people away from Trev, holding a balloon in her hand. She was squeezed between an old lady and a short guy in thick glasses. They were all posing and laughing.

Beth didn't go to their welcome party, Any did. It looked like she had a lot of fun there. Beth didn't regret not going. She always felt awkward during these kinds of events, surrounded by people she didn't know. She never understood how to make small talk about random stuff. Any was a pro in that... that's why she went to a party.

Beth stuck Any's photo to a board and hid it back in her closet. Years of adjusting, moving from one place to another and the system was finally working well. They stayed in this apartment for over a year and no one noticed anything suspicious.

"We might be more careful with lenses and hair though..." Beth said to herself in the mirror while brushing teeth. "Maybe not... normal ladies change looks sometimes... We'll be fine. I'm too paranoid again."

Beth heard someone knocking on the door. She put her robe on and rushed to open it. Tall skinny guy wearing a long coat and ripped jeans looked at her like he didn't expect to see her.

"Trev!" Beth smiled as wide as she could, trying not to look fake.

"Hey, Beautiful!"

Trev was standing next to the big friendly looking dog. Beth always felt particularly paranoid about animals feeling that something was wrong. Dog looked like she suspected something, but was not interested in investigating it. Beth smiled even wider, feeling relieved. Last thing she needed now was for the dog to start barking at her.

She looked at Trev's smiley face again. He looked neater than in the picture. His hair was pulled in a ponytail, colors of his clothes were matching this time, sneakers were a bit worn out though.

Beth realized that she never replied to his greeting and corrected herself:

"Hi Trev. How is it going?"

Wow, that sounded casual. Deep inside Beth was really proud of her acting skills.

Trev stretched his hands holding something wrapped in gray paper and orange rope: "I have something for you!"

"Wow, really?" Beth didn't need to fake that reaction. It was totally natural.

"Remember you said that I need to draw a picture of you one day?"

"I was... joking..." Beth was bothered with the perspective of posing for a picture. "You don't need to waste your time on drawing me. You probably have so many requests..."

Beth was trying not to be judgy of a guy that is making his living by drawing pictures.

"No, I did it already!"

Beth took a package from his hands not knowing what to do next. Trev felt her doubt and said: "Just open it. If you hate it, just say so. I got used to getting criticized a lot."

For a moment Beth felt sad for him, but then she realized that a few minutes ago she was judging him for not having a proper job. Apparently she was not the first.

Beth hesitated for a moment and then with one sharp movement ripped off the cover of her gift. She looked at it speechless.

Inside a wooden roughly golden colored frame was a picture of Any made only with fall colors. There were only outlines, but she could clearly recognize her with that messy hair and bright eyes...and that scarf of course. It was stunning.

"It looks so... beautiful. She is so..."

Trev interrupted: "You mean you. It's you in the picture".

Beth bit her lip, smiling nervously: "Yeah, I mean me. It looks so much like me! I'm just confused. You're really talented!"

"You sound surprised!"

"No, I'm not!" Beth smiled even wider.

"I posted it on my social media already and all my followers want to know who is in the picture. But I will keep it a secret, don't worry. I don't want them to invade your privacy or something... "

"Followers..." Beth had a hard time thinking that Trev might be famous and followed by anyone.

"Yeah, not much... just a few millions..."

"Few millions..." Beth was holding the picture frame so tight now only hoping that it could handle the pressure. "Oh, I got so stunned that I forgot to thank you! No one has ever drawn a picture of me before!"

Trev was blushing: " Thanks for the inspiration..."

He realized that it became awkward and excused himself shortly. Beth was standing next to the closed door for a while, holding the picture in her hands.

"Oh, Any..." Beth covered the picture back in gray paper as neat as she could and tied an orange rope back at it.

"Just like new!" she said sarcastically looking at the obvious ripped corners and scotch tape all over it.

Beth put a gift on a nightstand, took a notebook from it and started writing:

"Hi Any,

No worries, of course you can have a day! I know how in love you are with autumn. Let's say Saturday... It should be quiet.

Trev came by. He caught me by surprise. He drew a picture of you. Have a look. Sorry I had to open it in front of him, so the packaging is not as original."

Beth was staring at the empty page of paper below her writing. How to put it right? How to tell her to be careful without being a control freak again? How to put it in words that will not upset her? Oh God, Any was so fragile and sensitive. Beth always had something to say but with Any she had to stop herself, rephrase and analyze. Beth wondered if Any was doing the same while writing to her. Beth looked around the room hoping that something would help her. She looked at the door. No one ever stepped inside her bedroom. For the last year only herself and Any were seen by these walls. It was not safe to invite people, they could see something... it happened before.

Beth thought of Trev again, how he was standing in the hallway just a while ago. She didn't invite him in, didn't offer coffee. Should she? What would Any do? He came to see Any at the end of the day.

Beth looked at the closet. Their secret was behind that door. Were they careful enough? It's been one year and no one noticed. She was just paranoid as always. Beth decided not to write anything else and put the notebook back. She nodded to herself with appreciation. She was working on herself and it was not easy not to get carried away. She scrolled in her mind the scene from earlier. Trev with his awkward smile and dirty shoes... was cute and definitely talented. Beth nodded to her own thoughts again. The idea of finding him not frustrating was surprising to her.

"I am changing after all!"

She looked at herself in the mirror. Black dress and boots, dark gray coat, even her hair looked darker now, moistened with gel ant put in a tight bun. There was no single trace of bright color on her.

"Or not changing that much..."

Beth realized that she put everything on automatically. This was her style, her colors, her routine. She looked at the gift left for Any by Trev and wondered how he would draw her picture. In gray and black colors? Or knowing her, he wouldn't even be inspired to draw... But if he would be though, Beth would love to see this picture. Beth smiled.

"What the hell is wrong with me?"

She put her thoughts behind and exited the apartment, trying to stop scrolling through the images of Trev in her head.

Any

3...2...1...

Any removed her stranded hair locks from her face and looked at the window. Sunlight was streaming through it. Her eyelids were burning.

"Oh, Beth... You need to stop staring at that laptop or whatever you're doing with those eyes! It's painful after all!"

She rubbed her eyes, but it didn't help at all. She dropped her face back to the pillow.

3...2...1...

"I will not waste this beautiful day complaining about my eyes hurting! Suck it up, Any! We're stronger than this!"

Any jumped from the bed almost losing her balance and slipping on the carpet edge. She giggled thinking how lucky she was not to fall and break something.

"Gracious!" She said bowing at her own reflection in the big mirror. "Good start!"

Any saw a reflection of something orange in the mirror. That color looked out of normal for this room. She turned around and jumped in the bed again, trying to reach the rope like a cat. She pulled it to herself so hard that a rope got almost untied and a gift almost flew away from her.

"Almost!" She commented to herself.

She looked at the notebook on a nightstand, thinking that she probably should read it first. Beth would not leave a gift without any reason and explanation.

Any bit her thumb, flashing through important dates in their life.

"Did I forget anything?"

Beth always had a reason for a gift. Spontaneity was not her strongest part. And this one didn't look like she packed it.

Any quit guessing and opened a notebook on her knees.

She read through the neat cursive excitedly as fast as she could and threw the book aside.

"Oh, Trev!"

She ripped the packaging apart and stopped for a moment stunned. It was her picture and she loved the way Trev saw her. Picture was the brightest thing in the room. Orange and yellow colors were glowing in the sunlight. Any touched the surface and realized that there was no glass in a frame and she felt its texture with her fingertips. Smooth paint on rough paper.

Any hugged it, picture frame squeezed to her chest. Sharp edges scratched her skin mildly, but it was worth it. Any looked at the scratch patiently, pronouncing the diagnosis:

"No blood! And again, we are ok! Nothing is going to spoil this day!"

Any was the only one who got hurt, fell or scratched. She often lost her balance or stumbled.

"What did you expect? I have access to this body almost never compared to you! It's hard to navigate and not to hurt myself!" She wrote angrily in a notebook after Beth found another bruise. She didn't understand... of course, how could she? Beth had everything under control and Any was the only weak point, the only uncontrollable mess in her life.

Any smiled thinking how long it took to reach the level of understanding they had now. It was far from perfect, but now at least Beth was not blaming her for bruises.

She remembered the time when she was craving for a tattoo and how Beth resisted. Any pulled a colorful knitted sock from her right feet and rubbed a line tattooed on the edge of it. In a beautiful curvy script it was written "I climb the tree to see the world".

Beth hated sandals, flip-flops or anything that was showing her feet which she considered ugly. Even in summer heat she was wearing something that was hiding every inch of them. She would wear socks on the beach if she could. Any giggled. Not like Beth was going to a beach often. Any looked at her tattoo again. It was something hers, something that belonged only to her. After all these years she loved every inch of it and never regretted doing it.

"It's time to climb a tree!"

Any rushed to a closet, took a bunch of stuff out of it and threw it on bed. Normal ladies were complaining that they have nothing to wear. Any had an opposite issue. She had too many clothes and not enough time to wear them. Beth was never stopping her from shopping. Any always got everything she wanted despite the fact that she was not making money. Beth was paying. It was mutual agreement and both of them were OK with it.

Any looked at the pile of clothes, funky and colorful. She wanted to put it all on and to look like a Christmas tree, but common sense took over. Sky blue jeans, striped sweater, orange coat and boots. And of course a huge orange scarf and fingerless gloves. Any looked at herself in the mirror, happy and satisfied. Her copper colored hair was shining and looked like she was recently electrocuted.

"Let the fun begin!" She fetched a backpack from the floor and rushed outside.

It was beautiful. Sun was covering everything around with its gentle touch, most of the trees had their outfits changed to autumn party. Air was still warm, but fresh. Just enough to wear a light coat and still be able to feel summer touching your skin for a last time.

Any had a long way to go. She pulled a folded piece of paper from her pocket. The list was written by her hand, most of the points crossed out of it. She pointed her finger at the one of the pending ones, which was saying: "Eat lunch on the top of the mountain".

After more than two hours of riding in the train and climbing the mountain, Any finally was standing in the desired place. It was simply breathtaking. It was on the edge of a mountain covered with autumn. She saw all her favorite colors everywhere. It felt like autumn was hugging her.

"Colors of my soul..." Any felt like crying. It was one of the best views she could remember. She spread her hands breathing deep and imagining herself flying over this beauty: mountain covered with trees, glowing river stream. For a few moments Any was standing like this with her eyes closed, just taking it in, enjoying precious freedom. It lasted like forever, but it was still not enough. It was never enough.

She heard something behind her, but was not in a rush to open her eyes. Just thought: "Probably a squirrel... not worth my attention now..."

Suddenly "squirrel" coughed apologetically. Any turned around fast, almost slipped. After finally gaining her balance back she looked in the direction of a noise.

She looked at him, he looked back. He was standing there apparently for a while with his shoulder pressed against the nearby tree. He was watching her and was not hiding it. Tall and thin, with dark hair covering his ears, pale, even too much for a normal person. It contrasted with his hair and black long coat. His eyes looked gray and lifeless, Any noticed dark unhealthy circles under them. He looked like he was recovering after a severe illness.

Any smiled thinking that it was exactly how she imagined Man in black from the "Dark tower", the book she was reading for years now.

He saw her smile and mild confusion ran through the pale face. It lasted for a moment than he pronounced with a voice good enough for movie narration:

"You took my spot." He pointed at the log next to Any, which looked quite convenient to sit on and enjoy the view.

Man didn't sound like he had any single emotion about this case. Any smiled even wider now and pronounced imitating his deep and lifeless thone:

"You ruined my moment! Was it that hard to wait until I finished?"

"Finish what?" Now he looked irritated.

"Finish whatever I was doing! Didn't you notice that I was busy?"

"You were just standing there..."

"Not important enough? Oh, sorry for ruining your plans of sitting on the log!"

Any took her backpack from the ground and started to pull a blanket out of it. He was not saying anything, just watching her struggle. Frustrated, Any pulled so hard that accidentally scratched her finger with a zipper. Blood drops appeared on it almost immediately. Any put the finger in her mouth, so the drop will not fall on the blanket. He looked worried now.

"Are you ok?" He asked softer now. "Do you need help?" It sounded like a peace offering.

Any was not going to accept his apologies that easily.

"I got this..." She opened a backpack pocket and started to pull her emergency aid kit out of it: sanitizer, bandages, healing cream.

Man giggled.

"I see, you got this... all pharmacy is in."

"How were you going to help exactly? Sarcastically commenting on my first aid kit?"

Within a few quick steps he appeared right next to Any and in a second was holding her bleeding finger in his hand. Any was so surprised with this quick move that she didn't think of pulling her hand away. She just mumbled:

"Your hands are cold." It was true, she barely felt his skin through this stunning cold.

"Better for your bleeding finger." He was moving fast, cleaning the cut and applying bandages, like he did it thousands of times per day.

"Will I live, Doctor?" Any smiled and looked up to the cold eyes.

He pushed his stranded hair back with his hand and stepped back in the direction of a log, taking the blanket from the ground and spreading it over the log.

"If you have something to live for..."

Any didn't see his face, but felt his sad smile while he was saying it.

"I can think of something." She watched him sitting on the blanket. Weirdly enough, she didn't have any objections. She took her backpack from the ground once again and pulled a lunchbox out of it. She went straight to the log and seat so close to a stranger that he had to pull his coat from under her. Any ignored this action, while being busy with pulling soda cans out of her bag. She stretched her hand and it ended up in the stranger's hand. She almost dropped it as he pulled away not expecting something cold and metal to touch his palm. He caught the can on its way to the ground.

"Good reflexes!" Any mentioned, pulling other can out of the bag.

She looked back at the stranger. He was staring at a soda can.

"I haven't seen this drink since high-school..." He said quietly.

"It's not easy to find, but there is one spot in the Kingsgate with a bunch of stuff..."

He interrupted her "You travel to another state to buy soda?"

Any nodded, taking a sip: "Definitely worth it!"

He took a sip from his can and a sarcastic smile appeared on his face again.

"Thank you..." He said quietly, almost apologetically.

16

"Just a pay back for saving my finger." Any giggled. He smiled again.

Any opened a food container and hit a stranger with her elbow gently, offering him to get food from it.

He took one small dumpling from it and put it in his mouth. Any did the same. She nodded happily realizing how hungry she was and how satisfying it felt now.

After a few minutes of silent chewing, Any started talking: "Are you going to stay for a while? If you are, I can leave the blanket..."

"Are you going already?" He sounded disappointed, Any loved this new tone of his voice.

"I'm done here. I had lunch on the top of the mountain. Oh, I forgot! Can you take a photo of me?" Any pulled her camera out of the backpack.

He took it from her awkwardly, the same way he did with a soda can. Any jumped from the log a few steps ahead, almost to the edge, fluffing her hair on the way, so it looked even more wild and messy now. She spread her hands the same way as she did when he first saw her, only this time she was facing him.

Stranger looked at her face through the camera. This smile was so wide and genuine, these eyes glowing with weird orange cracks, weightless hair flying in all directions. He pushed the camera button. Any jumped back at him, pulling the photo from his hand, eager to see it.

"I love it! Thank you! So I'll be going..."

He interrupted, worried that he would not have a chance to squeeze his words into her speech.

"Stay..."

17

"This will be a terrible waste of time!" Any pulled folded paper and a pen out of her pocket and started scratching out one of the sentences. She didn't even realize when the paper stopped being in her hand and appeared in a stranger's.

"It's a list..." He declared staring at it for a few seconds.

"I know..."

"It's a bucket list." He declared again.

"Secret bucket list." Any said mysteriously and laughed.

"Not that secret anymore." He smiled again.

"You look better when you smile." Any was proud of her observation.

"I don't do it much."

"Oh, really?" Any laughed again.

"So... are you planning to finish this list today? That's why you're rushing?"

"Today? Are you joking? I hope to finish it by the end of the year!"

"What's there to finish?" He looked at the list again, with more attention this time.

For the first time since they met, Any looked upset and he noticed it.

"Oh, sorry, for disappointing you with my easy to do list!" Any was angrily pushing her staff back in her bag when she felt his ice cold hand on hers again.

"I didn't mean it."

She looked at the stranger and she believed him. He didn't mean it, he didn't know, he couldn't imagine... It was a genuine mistake. She felt his palm getting warmer, like he was charging with her hot and sweaty hand. She felt his skin now. Idea ran through her head. It was the first time someone held her hand like this. It was weird.

"I know." She simply said looking straight into his cold eyes. "I really need to go now."

"Why are you upset?" His tone was rough and cold now, the same one he used to blame her for taking his spot.

"I'm not going to spend more of my precious time talking with you. I took your spot, remember? Time for you to enjoy it the way you wanted, without me."

Any took her backpack and rushed away. After few steps she turned around and said with a smile to a stranger sitting on her blanket:

"I hope you find something to live for."

He did not reply. Only when she disappeared in the woods he said quietly:

"I hope I will."

Beth

Beth was sitting behind her work desk, tapping her notebook with a pencil. She was thinking about it since morning. Any was hiding something from her. She read a large and colorful story in their notebook today, browsed through a bunch of autumn photos, but couldn't get away from the feeling that something was off. For the first time in months Any didn't ask to go out. Any was definitely depressed and hiding it. Beth was scrolling through all the similar moments in their life. It was almost impossible for her to understand what was going on, because she didn't know what happened yesterday.

Beth took a deep breath and released the air as slow as she could. It was cruel. Any could pop up any time and see things with Beth's eyes, but she never did it. Beth, on the other side, would kill for a chance to take a glimpse on Any's life, but she couldn't. It never made sense to Beth. Control freak was cut of an opportunity to control and free spirit was not willing to be completely free. Any was out only during sleep time sometimes, just to read their notebook, to keep herself updated. Beth always knew when it happened. First, she was waking up sleepier than normal. Second, she was finding small apologetic noted in a diary. Third, there was always something out of order. Or Any's knitting kit was moved, or her book. Any was not physically capable to keep things in specific locations. That's why they had their lives separate. Beth couldn't stand her items to be moved around, but she could tolerate Any's book jumping from table in living room to night stand or even kitchen drawer.

Beth decided to ask Any regarding yesterday, but didn't know how to without hurting her fragile soul.

"Busy?" Face appeared without knocking in a space between door and door frame.

"That depends..." Beth was not in the mood to pretend to be friendly.

Les smiled ironically.

"Moody, huh? Something happened yesterday?"

"I wish I knew!" Beth was going to exclaim, but didn't and just nodded with a guilty smile.

"So bad that you decided to skip a meeting?" Les found her reflection in a mirror on the wall and started to comb her hair with her fingers. Measure was completely unnecessary as her hair looked simply perfect already. Platinum blonde with dark roots, straight, glossy and long. Beth could only wish to have locks like this instead of her mess.

Les always looked like she stepped from the cover of a fashion magazine. Impeccable taste in clothes and accessories, perfectly balanced makeup. But to put away the perfect look, Les has a good soul and a unique sense of humor. Les was the closest to a friend Beth ever had.

Les finished staring at the mirror and looked at Beth again noticing her confusion.

"Meeting... the one we should attend to hear updates regarding the new owner. No worries, you didn't miss anything important! Just half an hour of useless speech from Swen..." Les cleared her throat trying to do a best impression of the CEO. "You don't need to worry, nothing will change with the new managing company. Just keep doing a good job!"

Les started to cough and laugh at the same time.

"Yeah, right! New owner will just come and change nothing. Was it ever like this?"

Les looked at Beth expecting an answer this time, but not patient enough to stop expressing her feelings. She continued talking:

"People talk. I heard this new owner is always putting his trusted people in charge. He has a mind of a genius, creative as hell and way much more technologically educated than normal people of his age. Yes, he is in his 60s. He has a bunch of ex-wives and kids, who will inherit his billions."

"Did they say it at the meeting?" Beth couldn't hide irony.

"Of course not! I told you that the meeting didn't give me new information. I have my sources!" Les stopped pacing through the office and dropped herself in the guest chair next to Beth's desk.

Beth was not impressed at all. Les knew everything about everyone. She had perfect memory and used it as her biggest value. You could ask Les if she answered the call from specific person few years ago and she would literally quote what she heard from the caller. You would never see her writing notes or carrying notebook. She was paid more than most of colleagues in the office and everyone knew why.

Les kept playing with the ends of her hair while saying:

"But you're going out with us tonight, aren't you? Don't tell me you forgot about it also!"

Beth bit her lip. No one invited her to go. It was normal as people stopped inviting her out, tired of endless excuses.

"Karl will be there." Les added this note hoping that it will convince Beth to go.

"Since when am I liking Karl so much to go out with him?"

"You don't." Les smiled and winked. "He does... he called you genius, he never does it. You know how hard it is to impress him?"

"He is my superior, my job is to impress him."

"I'm not talking about work, babe! He looks at you, like he wants, hmm you know, to get to know you better." Les winked again.

"Is it your hobby to try hooking up people?"

"No, but I'm darn good at it. I know people, you know... And when I say that Karl likes you, I can guarantee it. Anyway, don't you want to gossip about the new boss?"

"Can't wait!" Beth exclaimed sarcastically.

"Oh, you. That's why you don't have a boyfriend Beth! You're just being a boring old lady now!"

This kind of teasing was normal between them and Beth didn't take it personally. Instead she beated Les with her own weapon:

"So if you are so cheerful and fun, why don't you have one?"

Less looked at her own reflection again.

"Well said, Bethany! I have a very simple explanation for you: none of men can handle me and stand my brilliance. Just waiting for the right match."

"I'll let you know if I see anyone riding a white horse..."

"I prefer more practical vehicles actually... I'm serious Beth! You should come, drink beer, have fun and forget about whatever is bothering you!"

"I'll think about it."

"The most I can ask for!"

Next morning Beth woke up with a headache. Was it alcohol from last night, or Any appearance overnight? Deep inside Beth hoped for the second option.

It was actually not bad yesterday. Les was talking a lot as always. It felt a bit awkward to be next to Karl, especially after Les shared her observation, but it was quickly fixed by a glass of wine. Beth was not much of a drinker, but she often admitted that alcohol helps a lot. To clear her mind, to calm down internal fears and endless paranoia. It was like a therapist who was not trying to fix her or share advice. But no matter how tempting it was, Beth couldn't drink often, it was not worth it. Even after one glass most of the time she was waking up with a piercing headache.

"Oh God..." She said, rubbing her forehead. "You never learn, Beth!" She put her glasses on an opened notebook, hoping to see funky handwriting in it. Nothing, crickets... Beth took a deep breath, holding a pen in her hand. It was time to do something about it, but the correct words were not appearing in her foggy mind. Beth dropped her face on the pillow and screamed loud enough to relieve stress and quiet enough for neighbors not to hear her.

Any

It was the first time in years when Beth insisted for her to go out. Any was sitting in bed with the notebook opened, rereading Beth's note again and again. That didn't seem like Beth.

"Weirdo." Any thought and finally put the diary aside.

Or Beth was suspecting that something is wrong with her, or something was off with Beth.

"I guess, we'll never know..."

She just didn't know what to do with herself today. Even the weather was dull and gray, sunshine was not streaming through the window like last time. This kind of autumn weather Any barely enjoyed. She jumped on the bed and covered herself with a blanket completely.

"This might work. Boring day for a change..."

Few hours passed ...

"Beth sensed that something was wrong with me. Maybe she was right." Any said out loud. She was sitting in the living room covered with a blanket, surrounded with everything she liked: book, knitting kit, yoga mat, her favorite TV show was playing in the background. Nothing worked.

"I am allowed to be depressed sometimes... that's what it is I guess... never had it before. Interesting. Feels so not like me."

Any pushed all her stuff aside, exclaiming: "That is not how this day will go. We can fight it! Just need a goal and focus!"

For the next few minutes she was sitting staring at a fall leaves wreath hanging on a door.

"Conquer? I can't recall when I did it last time..."

Any bit her thumb.

She put her clothes and backpack on and stepped outside her apartment.

"Let the fun begin." She said to herself excitedly.

She walked wherever her path was leading her, if the signal was red, she turned and crossed the road whenever the light was green. She ended up tying her shoes on one of the bus stops on her way and the same moment the bus arrived.

Any smiled: "Wherever you lead me..."

She jumped in a bus without even knowing where it went. She never took it before. Any looked around, the route apparently was not that popular, there were only a few passengers apart from her. She sat next to the window, waiting for a new sign to come and direct her somewhere. For a while nothing was happening, passengers exited the bus one after another, Any ended up alone with a driver. He was taking a glimpse at her from time to time, maybe because he wanted to get rid of a last passenger and go home, maybe because she looked lost, continuously looking around. Road was unfamiliar, Any was having a really hard time recognizing the area.

"Good job Any, now you're lost..." She said to herself quietly and noticed how the bus driver looked at her again. After a few minutes he announced that the next stop would be the final one. Any stood up and approached him, realizing that now he will definitely think that she is crazy:

"Excuse me sir... Where are we?"

Driver issued a short laugh, assuming that she was joking. Any blushed and he realized that she was not. He said with a soft cracking tone:

"We're in Kingsgate miss. Are you lost?"

"Not at all! That is exactly where I need to be!"

Driver smiled, but didn't believe her. Anyway, she was not his issue anymore.

Any stepped on the street. She loved this feeling: scary, but so exciting.

"What do you want me to do now?" She asked without expecting any answer.

She just kept walking down the street looking for signs. Weather was depressing, a small rain was covering her face, but it was not enough for her to bother with an umbrella. She kept walking and searching.

Tired and wet, she finally pulled an umbrella from her bag. Now her vision of surroundings was limited, Any started to get grumpy.

"So you brought me all the way to another state, so I can soak in the rain? Not like I'm not enjoying it... I'd rather be at home under the blanket, sipping tea. Come on, show me!"

Nothing was happening. Any kept walking. She started to feel rain reaching her feet.

"If We get sick, it's on you!"

People rushing under cover looked surprised at a weird girl walking under the rain and talking to herself.

Any stopped stunned. There was a shop right in front of her with a neon lottery advertisement. Big bright letters were saying "WIN", but "W" was losing its power and blinking, so the sign ended up as "IN" most of the time.

Any smiled relieved.

"Now we're getting somewhere."

She walked in the shop. It was empty, a man at the counter greeted her and continued watching TV. Any started looking, but she was not quite sure what she was supposed to find.

She was casually browsing through shelves, picking up stuff she didn't need. Few cookies for a snack, chocolate bar... and stopped next to a drink fridge.

"Oh, they have it too." Any opened the fridge door and pulled out a few soda cans, her favorite, the one she was traveling all the way to Kingsgate to buy. She knew only one spot where it was still available, now she discovered another.

"At least now this journey is not useless." Any smiled to herself.

Cashier looked at her with more attention than before. Any grabbed a few more cans from the shelf, making her hands full and having a hard time walking back to the counter without dropping something. Cashier kept looking at her weirdly. Any smiled to him saying:

"You know, there's only one more place I know that is still selling this drink. It's quite rare."

Cashier looked at her soda cans than back at her puzzled than pronounced slowly:

"I guess you're talking about Earl's, it's on the other side of the city. We're sort of the same chain."

"Oh, that's interesting... now I know where to go if they run out of it."

Any had no intention of coming back here, she didn't even understand where exactly she was and she walked most of the way. Route to Earls was so much easier.

Cashier looked at her with precision that became creepy now. He was wearing very thick glasses, but apparently they were not working well for him anymore because it felt like he could barely see.

"I know it's weird to ask, but what color is your hair? It's hard to say now, it's so wet and dark."

Any smiled awkwardly. That was actually a weird question.

"It's ginger..."

"Oh! It's you then! I almost missed it!"

"It's me what?" Any started to think of an escape route as this conversation started to bother her.

"Girl from a mountain!" Cashier exclaimed happily!

"Excuse me?"

"I have something for you!" Cashier looked much more excited than Any now. He pulled an envelope from under the counter and gave it to her. It was only few words scribbled on the top of it:

"I found you."

Any's lungs stopped producing air, her heart was pumping so loud that she could hear heart beating through all her body. She just stood there, holding the envelope, until Cashier started talking again.

"That is one romantic man you have. I heard that he has been in every shop in a city, looking for that drink, I mean... looking for you. He said that it's the only thing he knew about you, that you come to a city for this specific soda. He left envelopes in every shop he found it and by every, I mean only Earl's and mine. No one else is selling it anymore. He's lucky that it's a small city and a drink is not quite a bestseller."

"He... what does he look like?" Any was finally gaining her speech ability back.

"Tall, pale, wearing all black... skinny. He said that he's looking for a girl he met at the top of the mountain, with ginger hair and dark eyes with orange cracks. I almost missed it because of this rain, imagine that! And also these glasses are not good anymore."

Any felt how the envelope in her hands was becoming moist because of her hands sweating.

"All the city was talking about you, you know. But then you didn't show up and it got quiet. I felt a bit sad for a guy though. He was trying so hard to find you, but it was an unrealistic shot if you ask me... especially now, when Earl is stuck at home with his broken ankle and that girl that is covering him barely removes earphones from her ears... She would never identify you, she doesn't care."

"Wow! That is... just one big coincidence that I came here..." Any just couldn't wrap her head around it, so huge it was.

Minutes later she was sitting on the backseat of the taxi on her way home, holding the envelope in her hands. She didn't open it. Only the idea how close she was from not getting it was stunning. Few steps in another direction and she would never reach the destination. Any smiled to herself. Getting this envelope was a reward for letting it go and trusting the universe to guide her. This was the first time she actually felt it's guidance. In all the rest of her journeys like this, nothing significant happened. Yes, she had fun, yes, she discovered something new, but this... it was special.

She opened the envelope. On the inside part of it was written with the same handwriting: "I think I found something worth living for. Join me."

There was a paper inside, it looked very professional, the paper was rough, with a golden logo imprinted on the top. Any started reading:

"You are invited for a lunch of a lifetime adventure: lunch on the top of the mountain!"

Below was written in a smaller script:

"This invitation is flexible, please call us to make a reservation."

Any knew this restaurant, it had the most stunning view in the city. It was very hard to get a reservation there as its capacity was small and there was an endless queue of people dreaming of going there, especially tourists in the autumn season.

Disappointed, Any stuffed the letter back to the envelope. After a few moments of thinking, she pulled it out again. It was impossible that she went through all this adventure to get the letter which she will not be able to use. It didn't make sense.

She pulled her phone out of the pocket and started dialing the number written on the letter. The lady with a soft voice responded, Any heard a noise of the busy restaurant in the background.

"Hi there." Any started, her voice was shaky. "I just received a letter, inviting me for lunch in your Restaurant.

With the routine tone lady said:

"Wonderful! We're looking forward to welcoming you here. May I know under which name the reservation was made?"

"You mean my name?"

"Your name or the name of the person who invited you..." after a moment of silence the lady on the phone added: "It should be written on the invitation..."

"It's not..." Any felt the confusion she is causing to the lady. "I actually don't know his name... and he doesn't know mine."

That sounded weird. Lady on the phone was obviously not sure what to say. With a slight confusion she repeated slowly: "Let me just clarify, miss. You received an invitation from a person whose name you don't know and who doesn't know yours."

"That is correct." Any realized how unrealistic it was and smiled.

"Let me just connect you to my manager. Please hold."

It was a few minutes of silence and then Any heard a male voice which sounded unexpectedly excited.

"Good afternoon miss! Such a pleasure finally hearing from you! My apologies for the confusion of my colleague before, she was not aware of the current situation."

"I understand why she was confused. I would be too." Any smiled.

"Anyway, we're very happy that you called. When would you like to join us for your special lunch?"

Any paused. She didn't even think that she had options.

"Saturday...or Sunday... I'm not sure on which day you have availability. "

"Oh, don't worry about it! We can keep your table on both of these days and you can come any time when it is convenient for you!"

"Aren't you guys busy?" Any couldn't hold her surprised tone. From what she heard about this restaurant, it was packed and there was a huge waiting list for every day.

"Oh, extremely! Especially now for the autumn season as we have the best view in the state!"

Something was not adding up in this scenario and Any was quiet for a moment. Manager continued , feeling the need to explain the rip in logic: "But it is a very special case for us and you're the most valuable guest we expected in years."

Now Any was even more confused. She looked at the taxi driver who was obviously interested in a conversation and was sneaking out at her in the mirror.

"Oh, I appreciate it. Sorry for my confusion, I just didn't expect something like this. I'll try to come on Saturday, or on Sunday. Sorry, I can't be so sure now."

"As I said, we'll keep a table for you on both days just in case! Just ask for a Manager as soon as you arrive and I will be there for you!"

"Sounds good." Any said, still confused, and ended the call.

Beth

Now it was confusing. Beth couldn't believe her eyes. First she was chasing Any to take a day and now, she finally took one and straight after it was asking for another day. Her handwriting was so excited that it was almost impossible to recognize. Words were going in all the directions, some words were crossed out and replaced with others. It was obvious that Any had a hard time finding the right expressions to describe how she felt and also struggled to describe only a certain part of a story. She was hiding something again. But Beth was happy to notice that her mood had changed.

Beth put her notebook back into her bag. She rarely took it with her to work, but today she was almost late and didn't have time to read it.

She stood up and went to Karl's office. He was on the phone the time she was pretending to knock into the opened glass door. He gestured to her to come in and sit in the visitors chair. Beth waited. He was listening to a person on the phone, scribbling something on a bright sticky note. Beth noticed the way he smiled when he saw her. It was different than before that outing. Something clicked between them that day, but nothing actually happened. He was extremely professional, treating her the same as others, everything was as always, apart from this smile and mild blush of his cheeks when he saw her.

Beth was never giving herself a chance to think about Karl as a man. He was her boss and that was a step too high for her to ignore. It was against rules and Beth hated not following rules. But since Les planted that seed in her mind, she started noticing things she didn't before. She liked the way Karl looked. He didn't have a perfect body, was not tall or slim, but there was something about it... Beth liked the way he looked in a suit, it was obviously tailored and you could see how much attention was put into details, so the suit didn't make him look uptight or awkward, it complimented every inch of his body. Beth caught herself thinking about how he looked wearing normal clothes.

Karl finally ended the conversation and Beth came back to reality, almost forgetting what was the main reason for her to come here.

"What can I do for you Beth?"

"I just got last minute arrangements. I know I said I will be available on Saturday, but..."

"Oh, it's absolutely fine. Not to worry. You've been working so hard lately, you deserved a day out! Going on a network free mountain hiking trip again?"

"Aha..." Beth was surprised that she didn't even need to create a story. "Love those trips, so relaxing! It I so useful to feel disconnected sometimes..." Beth smiled hoping that he's buying it. She was lying, being disconnected was a terrible way of rest for her. Without her phone or laptop nearby she felt like she didn't have her hands. It was like being punished. Being disconnected for a day sounded like a nightmare, but it was a perfect alibi for Any's day.

"One day we will do it together." He said and Beth noticed that slight blush on his cheeks again. "The day when this company will not need at least one of us available on the phone at all times."

He didn't mean that. They both knew it. He said it only to pretend that it was still about work, not about them. They both knew it was not true anymore.

Karl made a fist with his left hand, almost invisibly touching his wedding ring with his thumb. Beth pretended not to notice. She also was trying not to recall her recent conversation with Les about it.

"So what, that he is married?" Les said, sipping coffee from a huge mug in her office. "I've dated married guys before and it was great! Married men treat you so differently."

"I can't believe I hear it from someone who believes in a perfect relationship."

"I believe in many things Beth, but I'm smart enough to understand that none of them might happen to me." Les said with an expression that looked optimistic and dramatic at the same time. "Don't get me wrong, Beth. I'm not forcing you to do anything that is against your code. I'm just sharing observations of the things which are obvious lately."

Beth was not arguing: "Do you think others notice?"

"People talk. Some of them care too much, few don't care at all. We're working in the office that is a homeland to so many gossips, but it doesn't mean all of them are true. Anyway, Karl is doing a great job hiding it..."

Seeing Karl touching his ring now made Beth feel funny. She was an expert in hiding things, he didn't need to explain how hard it was for him. The difference was, Beth was hiding another lifestyle, another person, but she was still able to be herself and to express her feelings. He couldn't. This ring was limiting his emotions, his desires and opportunities. For a moment Beth felt sad for all the people in marriages, who can't be 100% themselves anymore, who always need to take into account their partner. Beth did look after Any though, but whatever ridiculous it sounded, she was not uptight by this.

But now Beth was wondering how their life can change soon. Any obviously was hiding something. What if it was a guy? What if she falls for him? What if Beth finds someone? How will they figure it out?

Beth shook it off, feeling that panic attack was approaching. It was not a good time to think about it. Not at work, where she is so vulnerable.

"Too early to panic. It's still under control, Beth." She said to herself quietly.

Any

It was really breathtaking. Any took a few minutes to pull herself together. She kept walking with a camera in her hands, experiencing internal struggle. One part wanted to take photos and relive this memory over and over forever, the other part wanted it to be exclusive. Only now, only for her. Any felt greedy for this view.

She hid her camera in a backpack and looked at a restaurant. It looked old and rusty, with a lot of wooden and copper decor elements. It was matching the view perfectly and it was visible how much effort was put into blending it into the nature which surrounded it. It was perfect. If Any didn't know where she was heading, she'd assume that it was a house of a mythical forest creature, which was meant to live there and to protect the beauty around.

She took a deep breath and opened the door. Restaurant looked bigger inside than it seemed from outside. Leather couches, wooden tables, huge floor to ceiling windows allowing you to enjoy the views. Place was zoned in a way allowing everyone to interact with the views, but not with each other. Drapes were separating tables from each other, giving every visitor privacy. It was a bit noisy though, music was subtle, people talked, waiters rushed around. Restaurant was lively and full.

Any approached hostess , not quite understanding what to say: "Hi. I was told to call your manager as soon as I arrive."

Hostess greeted her and without further questions ran off somewhere. Within seconds she came back, elegant looking gentlemen rushing in front of her, like he couldn't wait to meet Any. She felt like some sort of celebrity. He shook her hand firmly, introducing himself and asking to follow him.

Any was a bit shocked when they walked through the restaurant and exited through the back door. Scenic view opened up to her eyes again, even more stunning than earlier. Gentlemen in a suit bowed and pointed in a direction, giving her a clue that he was leaving now. Any thanked him and started to follow a narrow mountain path.

After a few minutes she saw a bench, covered with her blanket and a man sitting on it. He couldn't see her coming, he couldn't hear her footsteps as they were also hidden by the wind. When Any almost reached a bench, she suddenly stopped and pronounced:

"You took my blanket."

He turned around slowly, with a barely noticeable smile.

"You took your time."

"How long have you been waiting?" Any imitated shocked expression.

"It feels like forever."

"I never promised..."

He interrupted her:

"I know."

"What if I had a life supply of my drink at home and I never needed to buy more?"

"You don't seem like this kind of person..."

"Like you know me that well!" Any smiled, showing the stranger all her teeth, the same way Beth never did.

"I took my chances." He sounded sad.

Any walked to a bench and sat next to him. He looked exactly how she remembered.

"Nice view." She said after a few moments of breathing in the beauty of a mountain covered with autumn.

"Indeed."

"So what is it? View is cool, but don't tell me that you called me to eat lunch here. We did something like this before..."

"Mood killer." He said annoyed.

Any laughed and pulled her camera out of her bag.

"At least I can take advantage..."

She didn't have a chance to raise her camera and take a photo, feeling his cold fingers fetching her hand. She didn't have a moment to react as she ended up hanging upside down from his shoulder. He took her backpack in the other hand and started walking.

"What do you think you're doing?" Any exclaimed with building frustration.

"Kidnapping you." Stranger said like it was obvious. "Other way was to ask you to follow me, but I don't want to take chances on that. What if you say no, or even run off like last time?"

"So in your head the better way is to take me somewhere against my will? Are you joking?" Any felt blood rushing to her brain since she was hanging upside down. She hit a stranger's back with her elbow. Apparently it was painful as he tripped and almost dropped her.

"Stop acting out Gingerhead! You want this adventure more than you want to be let go. Admit it!" He sounded tired from carrying her.

Any kept quiet. Her defensive instincts were activated, but he was right. Under the surface she was extremely excited and curious.

"Which proves that I'm not mistaken."

Any bit her lip, he was right.

After a few moments of silent walking, he finally put her back on the ground.

He looked exhausted, his deadly pale face started having more lively colors, Any's face was red. They looked at each other and laughed.

"You're heavier than you look!" He said in between laughing.

"You're weaker than you seem!" Any commented.

They kept laughing.

When Any turned around she saw something she definitely didn't expect. The sky ride cart was right next to her, attached to the huge wire falling to the bottom of the mountain.

"No way!" She rushed to it, tripped on the stone and almost fell.

"Do you ever look at the ground while walking?" He asked, annoyed.

"Nah, it's too boring." Any said, making sure her feet didn't get hurt.

Stranger caught Any's amazed look at the sky ride again and smiled. He looked proud of himself.

"Worth living for, isn't it?" He asked.

"Look at you." Any laughed in his face. "Show off!"

Smile got erased from his face immediately.

"Oh, really! Isn't it the best surprise you received in your life?" He looked annoyed with the disrespect she was showing to all his arrangements.

"It is." Any admitted with a slight shoulder movement. "But stop behaving like I owe you something! You did it for yourself, just needed a company I guess. I can't believe I was your first choice though..."

"You were." His annoyance changed to a sad expression.

Any realized that she went too far.. Her tone changed to a softer one now: "So, Mr.Stranger, you invited me to stare at this thing, or we're actually gonna ride this babe?"

She saw a barely noticeable sparkle in his eyes. They were good.

He offered Any his cold hand and they both entered the cart. It was cozy inside. Couch, table, mini fridge. Everything you needed for a few hours. But the best part: the view was simply breathtaking. Any smiled, it was the best moment she ever shared with another person.

It was not awkward, they didn't talk and it was not weird at all. Any kept thinking about it, silently staring at the window of the cart, slowly moving down the mountain. It was moving so slow that she barely noticed the shift of the view. It was beautiful, she thought of words to express it and couldn't find them.

"I wonder what Beth would say", she thought and smiled to herself immediately. She imagined Beth sitting here instead of her, on the couch with a stranger staring at the view. Possible? Chances were slim.

Any felt that he's watching her and turned around. He was sitting in the corner of the couch, with a book in his hands. He didn't try to pretend that he was not staring at her, just kept doing it.

"You smiled. That's why I'm looking at you like a creep. You thought about something and smiled. What did you think about?"

"Do you really want to know?"

"No." He answered simply and turned the page.

"Why did you ask then?"

"Am I not allowed to ask questions now?"

Any issued a guilty smile. She caught herself thinking that she wanted to trust him, that she was craving to tell him a secret.

"Do you want to know the secret?" Any asked with a twinkle in her eyes, teasing him.

He looked back at her again with a plain expression: "Not really."

"What is wrong with you?" She was disappointed, folded her hands in front of her chest.

"You asked the question. I answered." He said, with a barely visible shoulder movement and added: "If you wanted to tell me, you wouldn't ask for permission. It means that you have doubts, so probably it is something you shouldn't share with me. You don't know if you can trust me, so you are just searching for confirmation. I didn't give it to you and now you're acting disappointed. You feel like you can tell me something because I'm a stranger, I'm like your neighbor on a train ride. You want to tell me something as you'll never see me again. So your secret will be safe. Am I right?"

Any bit her lip. She hated how easily he felt it. She never felt so predictable in her life.

"I am, I guess..." He was holding a page of his book with his index finger because Invisible wind was rushing to turn it.

Any felt like she was stuck in a labyrinth. There was no way to go. He figured her out so easily that she was craving to get out of his grip. He saw it, he felt every doubt and involuntary movement and it was terrifying.

He looked back at the page he was holding with his finger and said quietly: "I don't want to be a stranger on a train."

"Who do you want to be?" Any shoot without thinking, feeling her cheeks blushing.

"This is a conversation for another day." He said with a smile, turning the page, without even looking at her.

"I'm not the only one here, who has doubts about sharing." She said.

He pierced her with an angry look.

"You are not the only one who can read people." Any turned back to the window.

Beth

Beth opened a notebook and a bunch of colorful photos slid out of it.

"One productive day, I see..." She smiled ironically.

Beth read the colorful story twice, trying to find gaps and almost marking them with a pen, like a school teacher correcting mistakes.. Any was surely hiding something or someone...

"Oh Any." Beth took a deep long breath. "What on earth is happening?"

Any didn't ask for a day. That was a weird thing and one more unexplained gap.

Beth blindly stared at the window. She needed to understand, but there was no way to do it. Beth paused her deduction process for a moment. One thought appeared in her mind. She didn't tell Any about Karl either. Beth shook it off. There was nothing to tell. They just sat next to each other on that outing. It was tight, they were squeezed together and she felt the warmth of his shoulder touching hers. There was nothing to tell... but when someone left and there was way more space on the bench, people spread and they kept sitting, glued to each other. None of them wanted to move. There was nothing to tell... Beth kept repeating to herself, but a picture of

Karl touching his ring was interchanging with a memory of a mild blush on his cheeks.

"Shut it, Beth." She said to herself out loud. "There is nothing to tell."

She almost jumped in bed, the phone call felt so loud, piercing through the thoughts she was trying to get rid of.

It was Karl. It was a normal thing for him to call her early on the day off. It happened many times before. Beth picked up the phone. His voice sounded weird.

"Beth..." He said with the tone she never heard in his voice.

"Yes." She answered, trying to keep hers steady and normal.

"Can I come up?"

Beth realized that shock was building up in her mind as a lightning. He sounded quiet and confused.

"Come up where?" That was the only thing she could think of.

"...to your apartment."

He took a pause before saying it. She felt that it was so hard and out of normal for him. Beth jumped from bed and opened the curtains without thinking or trying to be discreet.

"It's not possible..." was pulsing through her mind like a broken record.

She froze. She didn't need her glasses to recognize him. Karl was standing across the road, looking at her window.

"Come." Beth answered fast. She didn't have time to think. Action should be fast. He could not be seen here. Talking him into leaving will take time if it was possible at all. She took the fastest route. He needed to come up as soon as possible, preferably before neighbors noticed him. She saw him putting his phone in his pocket and heading against the door. In a

46

second Beth already stood next to her apartment entrance, squeezing her forehead and fists to the door.

"What are you doing, Beth?" was now pulsing through her mind.

She heard his slow heavy steps on the stairs. And when he stopped next to her door, he said with a begging note in his voice: "Beth..."

She opened the door mechanically, trying to keep her gestures as cool as she could, trying to hide her heart beating so loud that she could clearly hear it, trying to smile. He was standing in the doorway with a bottle and his jacket in his hand. His tie was loose, his shirt was not fresh, same as his breath. He was drunk.

"Come in." Beth said, trying not to demonstrate her surprise.

He walked in the living room and sat on a sofa. Beth stayed next to the door. He was not saying anything. She went to the kitchen and brought him a glass of water, putting it in front of him on a coaster. He put his half empty bottle on the floor next to him.

"Beth..." He exhaled. His voice sounded rough and tired, he was breathing heavily.

"What happened?" She answered, feeling her voice cracking.

"Beth..." He exhaled again without looking at her. "I'm sorry Beth..."

Karl shook his head and dropped it at his palms. It looked like it was too heavy for him to hold it. He sat like this for a minute, then spread one hand and took a glass of water from the table. Beth was standing next to the couch, not knowing how to react.

"I'm sorry Beth..." He repeated again and his voice sounded sharper this time, ice cold water was sobering him up. "I shouldn't be here."

"You shouldn't." Beth nodded. She sounded confused and judging.

"I'm sorry Beth..." He repeated again.

"What happened?" Beth repeated softer this time.

For the first time he looked straight into her eyes.

"I don't know."

Beth sat on the chair next to him. She was seriously worried about him now. She never could imagine him being like this. He looked and felt like a different person now.

"I was out with guys..." He mumbled, forcing himself to remember, fighting through the blurred mind. He took another sip and his voice became clear again. "I was out drinking... with guys... I'm sorry Beth."

"Keep talking." Beth said sharply, ignoring his apologies.

He obeyed. "I think I had too much to drink."

"No kidding!" Beth thought, but didn't say anything.

"I was out. And then it was time to stop drinking and go home. I didn't want to go home. Not home, I didn't want to go home to her..."

He sounded so sad and broken, Beth started to feel a chunk in her throat. It was getting hard to breathe.

"I didn't want to." Karl continued. "So I kept drinking and then I realized that there is one person I want to go to... but it was late and I didn't want to wake you up. So I waited until morning. I shouldn't be here Beth."

"You shouldn't." Beth repeated, feeling tears filling her eyes.

"It felt so clear in my head, for the first time in a while. There were no questions, no limits, I just knew what I needed to do... I remembered your address from your personal file. I guess I knew I would need it one day."

He got quiet for a few moments. Beth just kept sitting, looking at him, hiding his face in his hands. For a moment she thought that he was crying. But then he looked at her again and she saw that he was not.

"It is so clear in my head Beth... I'm sorry, but I needed to come, I needed to see you, I needed to say it."

Beth closed her mouth with her palm, trying to stop herself from asking what he meant.

"I needed to say it, Beth. I want you. More than anything or anyone I ever wanted in my life. I want to be part of your life, I want to see you not at work, I want to call you when I want to talk to you, I want to touch you..."

Beth felt tears dropping from her eyes.

"I'm sorry Beth... I just couldn't hold it inside anymore. It's burning so badly, I can't stand it. Every time I see you, I don't want this moment to stop. Every time I don't see you, you're in my mind constantly. I can't focus on anything else. Every time I realize that I shouldn't think about you in this way, I want to kill myself..."

Beth's cheeks were now wet with tears. He dropped his face in his palms again. She was thinking only about one thing. He was never so real in front of her as he was now.

He started to breathe deeper, his face resting on his palms, being quiet for a while. He was falling asleep. He was drained mentally and physically. Beth stood up and came closer, touching his shoulder. He put his hand on top of hers, looking at her with half conscious eyes, silently begging to say something. Beth softly wiped her tears with her sleeve and said:

"You need to rest." She pushed his shoulder softly, he obeyed, laying on the couch, holding her hand with his.

Beth sat on her toes in front of him. He looked at her not realizing if she was real, or just a projection of his imagination. She touched his cheek with her fingertips, feeling his freshly grown beard. He smiled and dozed off, breathing deeply. When he loosened his grip, Beth took her hand back, stood up, took a blanket folded on the back of the sofa and spread it over his body.

Only one thought was pulsing through her head now: "There is something to tell now I guess..."

Beth didn't know what to do with herself. She took the notebook in her hands, thinking of writing, but it didn't work out. She didn't know how to arrange thoughts in her head, not talking about doing it on paper. She gave up on this after the third attempt.

She kept rounding in the apartment, trying to keep herself busy, while Karl was heavily breathing, hugging the sofa pillow.

After a few hours of useless walking from kitchen to bedroom, she finally stopped and looked at herself in the mirror. She looked troubled. Her hair was messy, she was still wearing pajamas, her eyes looked lifeless and watery. That didn't look like Beth at all.

"Pull yourself together, Beth!" She whispered to herself. "It is under control, it's in your hands now. You decide what to do next, so stop whining!"

Something caught her attention. She looked around. Her phone looked silent, Karl's phone was too far for her to feel its vibration. There was only one more option.

Beth opened Any's side of the drawer. Bunch of clothes were just piled up on the floor, like she was trying to hide it last minute. Her scarf slides outside slowly, forced with the door opening. Any's phone was laying next to her bracelets on the top of a tower made of shoe boxes.

"She forgot to switch it off..."

They were trying to switch off their phones when others were around. It guaranteed more privacy. Exception was made only when Beth was waiting for an extremely important call or email. Than Any's head was filled with a whole bunch of instructions and scenarios of how to answer and what to do, whom to pass the message to. It was very rare and extremely complicated to pull out. Any's brain was wired differently and even if she tried her best, she could easily mess everything up. That's why most of the time they kept their phones private. This time, Any must have forgotten to switch it off. She often did it, but it was the first time Beth heard it.

She took the phone in her hand, feeling its rough surface. It was covered with glitter and stones and all the sparkles you could imagine. It looked like someone mashed a unicorn and dunked the phone in it.

One more notification appeared on a screen so unexpected that Beth almost dropped the phone with surprise. Beth didn't expect the face recognition to do its job and phone to be unlocked so easily. She was facing the message screen now, opened automatically.

Beth cringed and whispered to herself:

"Good job Beth! Now you're invading Any's privacy. Can this day become even more complicated?"

It was a photo. Someone sent her a photo of a hand holding two tickets. Beth sport's knowledge was very basic, but she could recognize that it was tickets for a game.

Short text message was shown below. Only one word: "Interested?"

The phone number was unfamiliar to Beth and was not saved in Any's phone either.

Beth bit her lip. It was definitely a male hand. It was no Trev for sure. There were no bracelets on his wrist, no half scratched black nail polish. Just a pale gentle male hand and an edge of a black coat, or maybe shirt.

"Oh, Any..." Beth took a deep breath. "I hope you're in less trouble than I am."

Beth looked at the opened door to her living room, where Karl was uncomfortably stretched over the small sofa with his feet up and his hand dropped on the floor. Beth was not the one who could judge here, she had a drunk married guy sleeping on her sofa after admitting his feelings to her.

Beth looked at a photo again. Idea ran through her head swiftly. She opened the phone's gallery hoping for new evidence. Nothing. No more photos of a stranger. Beth felt guilty for being so curious about Any's life and at the same time not sharing hers. She took a pen and a notebook in her hands again, this time she will do it.

"I need to tell you something!" Les stormed into Beth's office so unexpectedly that she literally jumped In her chair.

"You are going to give me a heart attack one day." Beth commented, trying to hide her real emotions. She was terrified that now Les knows, or someone else from the office found out about her and Karl.

Beth took a big coffee cup from a table, took a sip and pronounced as distant as it was possible: "I'm all ears."

Les looked at the opened glass door, probably deciding if the gossip is secret enough to close it. She made a decision immediately, keeping it opened, but lowering her voice instead.

"Remember I told you that our new owner normally puts his people in charge of new projects?"

"How could I forget?" Beth secretly congratulated herself that gossip didn't include her or Karl this time.

"It's happening!"

"No way!" Beth's reaction was almost comical.

"Stop teasing me!" Les laughed softly, but artistically. Her eyes stopped at the mirror hanging on the wall, making sure she looked perfect at this moment of glory.

Beth waited for a moment for the beauty check to finish. Les looked back at her, whispering with the evil smile: "Don't you want to know who will be your new boss?"

Beth froze. Karl was her boss... they couldn't... horror squeezed her heart and she almost gasped for air. On the surface she demonstrated the most condemned, interested look. Les was getting what she wanted. She built the pressure.

"Not your boss actually, they're not going to replace anyone, who is potentially your secret boyfriend..." Les winked.

Beth realized that her lungs stopped producing enough air and she coughed in her fist theatrically.

"Karl is still at his throne, but now the owner's son will be included in a chain of command."

"What do you mean?" Now Beth's reaction was completely natural.

"They created a title for him. Somewhere in between Karl and Swen. No major function, just to sneak around and to sign specific papers."

"That's weird..."

"I know... But my sources report that it is the owner's regular routine. He always puts his trusted people, gets them involved... blah blah. But the interesting part here is that it never was one of his family members."

"Maybe he's feeling that it's time to retire and someone needs to take over eventually?"

"That was my first idea also!" Les exclaimed with her index finger piercing up in the air. "But there is something else behind it! I'm sure."

"We will find out soon enough I guess."

"I knew you would like it!" Les definitely overreacted on Beth's interest in this subject. She jumped off the chair and was already heading out of Beth's office, but turned around on her high heels with a suspicious look. "Your hair, it looks brighter today. Did you do something new with it?"

Beth swallowed the gulp in her throat as discreetly as she could, casually saying: "New conditioner... nothing major..."

"Nice." Less underlined, almost running away, urging to pass a fresh gossip to someone else.

Beth pulled a small pocket mirror out of her bag immediately and looked at her reflection. Her hair normally darkened with hair wax and pulled tightly in a bun did look different now. It looked more smooth and curls were more defined, one of them actually escaped the tight grip and was curling next to her ear. Beth made a mental note of it and pulled it back behind. She knew what Les was talking about. Her hair color changed slightly, it was brighter than normal. Beth was lying regarding the conditioner, she didn't change her hair routine for years now. It was something else. Beth realized something that made her heart beat faster. Her hair looked more like Any's now. She closed the mirror so hard that it could break inside. The silent question stuck in her throat.

Any

Any was sitting in bed, holding the notebook in her hands so tight that she felt her palms sweating and her nails leaving marks on the leather cover. That was intense...

"Oh, Beth..." She only said reading the emotional letter.

Her eyes were full of tears. Beth never was so open and emotional before. Any could feel every word like it was her own. Her heart was creating background music for intense reading.

"Oh, Beth..." Any repeated again. Her finger was sliding down the page, following the neat cursive that never looked this way either. Beth had so many feelings that she was rushing to record it as soon as she could. Her handwriting looked like never before.

Any reached the end and her expression changed. She looked at the door of her drawer and ran off to it, not realizing that her feet were stuck rolled in the blanket and falling on her palms from the bed.

"Oops. No, we're good." Any whispered, trying to get rid of the blanket grip. She won a battle, but her sock remained a prisoner.

Any stood back on her feet and rushed to a drawer, opened it widely and saw her scarf slowly sliding down on the bedroom floor. Beth put it back exactly the way it was. Any looked at the phone. There was a notification on the screen, which opened immediately while recognizing her face.

It was a message. Additional to the one that Beth described, apologizing for invading her privacy. Any didn't judge Beth. She would probably do the same in her place. She was absorbed with a message now and she didn't care what Beth thought about it.

She opened a photo and enlarged it to see the dates on the tickets.

"Sports..." She deducted with zero understanding what the game was and how important it was for its fans.

It expired, the ticket was dated two days ago. Any was disappointed, but only for a moment. Her attention was pulled by the next message.

"Interested?" It said,

Any scratched the back of her head. She was interested, she always wanted to go to a game, to experience the vibe of that crowd, to cheer for someone. Any didn't understand the rules of any game, but it didn't matter...

Next message was sent on the day of the game. It was a photo again. Photo of an empty seat, apparently on the same game. Message was added: "Lost your chance, Gingerhead. They won."

Any still had no idea who won and what the game was about.

She typed faster than she thought: "Show off." And hit send before realizing it.

Message was read immediately, like the only thing he was doing at the moment was holding the phone in his hand, waiting for her reply.

"I thought you gave me the wrong number." He answered.

"If I would, you'd still track me..." Any added laughing emoji.

"Weirdo." He replied.

"Stalker."

"Busy today?"

Any thought for a moment. She absolutely forgot what her plan was for today. She pulled a folded piece of paper out of her bag, reading through it, pretending there was something more important than what he was going to offer. She took her time and it felt like forever.

He was impatient.

"Oh, come on." He texted.

"What?"

"I noticed already that you're hard to get. Don't make it even harder."

"You actually are a stalker." Any left one more smiley face at the end of the line.

He didn't reply. She was waiting. Minutes passed. Any was pretending not to care, slowly walking to the kitchen and making coffee, but her palms were sweating. She looked at the phone casually, but with all her soul she wanted it to show one more notification.

Any thought about the emotional story Beth wrote for her. It felt weird. They both ended in trouble almost at the time. Apparently they were more alike than she thought.

"You're heartless."

Notification finally popped up. Then one more: "How can you ghost me so easily? How dare you?" For the first time he also sent her a smiley face.

"You're demanding." She replied. "I don't like it."

It was only partly true. From one side, Any hated when someone was needy or demanding, but from the other, deep inside she wanted it, especially from him. She was not going to admit it. Not yet, at least. She thought about it, wiping a milk she just spilled on a table.

"You can like it or not. I want to see you."

Any almost dropped her phone on the floor while reading it. It sounded so familiar. It sounded like what Karl said to Beth, or at least how she imagined it.

"I'm coming to your apartment."

Any hold her breath, it sounded even more familiar now. She pulled herself together and replied:

"You don't know where I live."

She added in her mind: "You don't even know what my name is... how hard can it be to find me?"

"I don't."

They stopped for a moment. One long and intense moment. He realized how impossible it is for him to locate her. She, breathing freely knowing that. Any appreciated the distance he was giving her. It was not matching with his pushy nature. It was obvious that he was doing something special for her, something extraordinary for him.

Few more moments of silence followed. Any glanced at the window, imagining how the stranger would stand on the street, like Karl did. She couldn't stop thinking about it. Karl...and Beth. So weird.

One more notification popped, pulling her from this thought:

"Please stop doing it."

"Doing what?"

"Disappearing."

"OK."

"Name the address and time, I will be there."

Any thought for a second and typed the address.

Silence followed.

"Pizza place? Seriously?"

"Best pizza in town!" Any texted with a wide smile which he was not able to see. She waited for a moment and added:

"Don't forget my blanket."

"I never forgot it, you did."

He was right. She did. She left it the first time, never expecting to see it again. She forgot it the second time, knowing that she will. There was no way back. She gave him her number, she signed an invisible agreement, saying that now he is not a stranger anymore.

She entered the diner with a wind, it was playing with her wild curls. Any saw him immediately. Sitting at the corner table, like a black stain in the colorful interior. She walked fast, enjoying the sound her new heels made on the wooden floor. She almost slipped, but he didn't notice. He was holding his phone in his hands, typing something with an irritated face.

She came close, put her purse on the bench opposite him. He finally looked up with a vivid smile.

"Stalking another victim?" She said with a teasing smile.

"Almost opposite." He answered with something that Any considered as a laugh.

"Do you ever wear something that is not black?"

She changed the subject so soon, he was not ready for it, but reacted fast: "Do you ever wear something that is not colorful?"

Any smiled and pulled her feet up, pointing at her new shoe sole. "Black!" She proudly exclaimed.

He created a sound which she considered as a laugh again. It was more similar to cough though.

"I have something for you." Any dived into her purse, it took her a while to find it.

He was looking at her, not knowing what to expect. She finally pulled out a thin knotted bracelet, made of orange, yellow and brown colors combined in weird wild lines. Any put it on a table in front of him with triumph.

He looked at a bracelet and back at her with a question mark in his eyes: "What is it?"

"It's a wish bracelet. You make a wish, tie it on your wrist and forget about it. When you lose it or break it, your wish will come true."

"Do I look like a five year girl to you?"

"Shut up and give me your hand." Any insisted.

He obeyed, against his common sense. He put his pale fist on a table in front of her. With a swift move Any covered his wrist with a bracelet and tied it.

"So now we're going to be friends forever?" He laughed, stretching his pinky in her direction.

"That depends on your wish!" Any was so excited about it that he couldn't say anything about it, just hid the bracelet deep under his sleeve.

"Now I like it!" He exclaimed looking at his wrist.

"Do whatever you want, just don't remove it!" Any was happy that he didn't reject it, which she assumed he would.

"They will take it off from my dead body."

"I hope your wish will come true before it."

He didn't say anything. Just looked at her with a trace of mystery in his eyes.

They were sitting on a blanket in the park. People around were doing the same with picnic baskets. Kids and dogs running around, digging themselves in darkened and crunchy autumn leaves. Everyone around was enjoying the last warm moments of the year. Park was filled with distant background noises. Any was busy, trying to cut the pizza with a plastic knife.

He looked at her with a charmed look. Even this small task was giving her so much joy. Her hair was so messy before that she pulled it in a messy bun, but a few stranded locks were still out, looking like antennas. Her colorful clothes matched the background. She looked like she belonged to this picture.

He broke a silence: "So where were you?"

Any looked up straight into gray eyes.

"You don't want to know."

"Secrets again?"

"If I tell you, I might need to silence you forever."

"You're getting pretty good at torturing me. I can understand being not available, but reading my messages and not replying for days. You're evil!"

"I do it all the time." Any nodded, not breaking eye contact with pizza.

She was lying, he noticed it. It was intriguing.

He already opened his mouth to ask, to investigate, but she looked straight up to the sky, distracting his way of thoughts. She put her opened palm up, like holding an invisible object. He noticed a small water drop landing on it.

People around were rushing, pulling together picnic supplies, fetching their kids and running under cover. Background noise changed to a rush. Any was just sitting with her palms spread up, waiting for new drops to come. He was looking at her amazed, shocked even.

"It's raining." She concluded, touching one of the rain drops on her palm, just to make sure.

He couldn't help but laugh, trying to play alone just to see how it would continue.

"It is." He said, putting his palm the same way.

Any looked around, disturbed impression rushed through her face. People were running, trying to get in their cars or to find cover elsewhere. Any looked at him. His hair started to get wet, small water drops were sliding down his coat. She smiled, as he was not saying anything, pretending that nothing was out of normal.

She pulled her hood up, covering her hair, which was already darkened by the rain. She spread her hand and took a pizza slice from the box, biting a piece of it with delighted emotions on her face. Stranger looked at her, not knowing what to think.

"Weirdo." He announced, taking a slice for himself.

"I'm not missing this rain, I haven't experienced it for so long." Any concluded, with mouth full, sipping coke.

"What are you talking about? It was rainy a few days ago."

"I know." Any said, staring at the tree, which was partly covering them from water drops.

She was lying and he knew it. There was more in this than he imagined, but he didn't ask. Deep inside he knew that he shouldn't ask, not yet.

Beth

Beth didn't feel nervous. Her mind was busy with other thoughts. She was sitting in Karl's office, looking at him gesturing, hearing him briefing her before the introductory meeting with the owner's son. He was not showing it, but she knew that he was stressed about it.

Beth couldn't help herself, she was present only distantly, hearing him like she was under water. Her mind was playing over the scene which happened after he woke up on her sofa. She was remembering how he woke up, took his jacket in his hand and just left without saying a word. Just looked at her with a sad and confused expression on his face and just left. Beth expected something totally different. She didn't even realize how she should feel about it. She just didn't know.

Karl behaved extremely professionally after it, even now, he was so absorbed with management updates. It was bothering everyone in the office. Les was sneaking from office to office sharing gossip, Karl was ready for an hour-long presentation demonstrating how valuable he was for the company. Only Beth didn't care. She was sitting in the office, tapping her pencil on the notebook, pretending to be absorbed with Karl's conversation. She was craving for clarity.

First, she wanted an explanation from him. Second, she wanted details from Any, which, once again, wrote a colorful story, briefly mentioning that she was out with the guy Beth doesn't know. And that was it. Beth spilled her soul on the paper, explaining to her the complications she was facing with Karl. Any was not ready to share yet. It was upsetting, but Beth understood.

"I hope hers is not as complicated as mine." Beth thought, nodding again to something Karl said. That sounded so ridiculous. It couldn't be easy for any of them. In the beginning maybe, but after. Beth took a deep breath, trying to chase away her panic attack. One stressed person in a meeting will be enough.

"You have nothing to be worried about." Karl said on their way to the new bosses office, thinking that her quietness is caused by stress.

Beth nodded. Deep inside she was pulled apart with 2 completely different desires: shake him out of this denial and just find out what the hell happened that day, or be quiet, obeying and peaceful about it.

"I'd rather go with the second option." She said to herself and nodded again.

He stood up from his big leather chair in a freshly furnished office immediately after seeing them in a doorway. Karl was in front, heading to a boss, stretching his hand in front of him for a firm manly handshake. He looked professional and cool. Beth was hidden behind him until he stepped aside to introduce her. She looked at the new boss and smiled, also stretching her hand to him.

How different it was. His handshake with Karl was so dynamic and friendly. But with her he just froze, forgetting to take her hand in his. For a few awkward moments he was completely quiet and didn't move. Beth was just holding her hand in front of him, looking into his gray eyes, which were simply staring back at her.

He realized how awkward it was after a few seconds, fetching Beth's hand in his both hands, like his life depended on it. Beth felt how cold he was, which was coming to a full picture with his extremely pale skin. Beth's hand was not much warmer either. She always had people commenting about it after a handshake with her. She thought that it might be the first time someone's skin was colder than hers.

He took her hand, but didn't stop looking weird at her.

Clearing his throat, he asked: "Have we met before?"

Beth felt how her hand mildly shook in his palms. She smiled again as friendly as was appropriate and answered: "I'm almost sure we haven't."

He nodded, confused. She was telling the truth and he knew it.

She noticed how unfocused he was during Karl's speech. Just nodded from time to time, like she did minutes ago with Karl. He turned to her casually looking, but she understood something was off.

Karl kept talking for a while, Boss was politely nodding, Beth was trying to figure him out.

After the meeting was done, the new boss stretched his hand again to shake Karl's hand. Small piece of orange knitted bracelet casually slides from under his black shirt sleeve. It was so out of character that Beth couldn't help but notice. She looked at the bracelet and a casual smile for a moment disappeared from her face. Stranger noticed it. She recognized it and he knew it. Barely visible twinkle lightened his lifeless eyes.

"Are you all right?" Karl asked her on their way to their floor from the boss's office.

"I am." She answered. All her internal power was directed on reducing the approaching panic attack. It could be a coincidence... that she looked familiar to the boss, that he looked at her this way, this bracelet. Coincidence only...

Beth reached her office, locked the door and dropped herself in a chair. She needed to know, but there was no way to find out. Any can be away for a week or even longer. Beth took another deep breath, trying to calm herself down. It was still early to panic.

When Les knocked on her door, Beth almost got a heart attack. Les opened the door and her smiley face appeared in a frame, saying:

"Hiding? Did you actually think that you could hide from me before telling the details?"

Les smiled and Beth felt how her heart shrinked in her chest.

Immediately after coming home Beth spilled her worries on the pages of their notebook. She described new boss with such precision that a photo robot could be made easily after reading it. She had so many question marks in her story, like she never had before. Beth caught herself realizing that she was never so interested in Any's life, never asked so many questions, never wanted her to show up so badly.

Normally they shared a general picture, information necessary for both of them to know. Like about neighbors or work, or friends. Beth realized that since they moved to this city they didn't have many friends. Normally Any was the one developing connections with people outside work, but after recent failures, Any significantly reduced her contacts... or so Beth thought. She knew about Trev briefly and that was it. Beth felt sad for a moment, realizing how much of her open and friendly personality Any did sacrifice for their safety. Yes, it was way much easier for her to be like Beth, much safer for them. Beth saw the paper of the notebook becoming wet, perfect cursive becoming crooked because of her tears washing it off. She touched a wet stain on a page not realizing what was happening. It was not a panic attack, not a Hulk mode when her frustration was overwhelming. She was crushed. Without hesitation she ripped the page out of the notebook. Beth never did it before. She shredded it in small pieces while her tears were flowing all over it.

She was thinking that maybe now it was her time to sacrifice her life and the world she created. It was Any's before, it was always Any's. Beth never actually realized it and she felt extremely selfish now.

"We can do it. I don't know how yet, but we will figure it out. It might not be that bad." She was saying to herself while tapping the pen on the empty notebook page.

She wrote it differently this way, holding herself from crossing the line. Instead of questioning, she described her experience with a light shade of anxiety. Stopping before putting every word on a paper, analyzing if it is light enough not to hurt a fragile soul.

It took hours to write and reread it many times. Beth was so absorbed in it like she was never before, so busy that she didn't see a new message on the phone.

It was Karl. Of course it was him. He definitely noticed the shift of her attitude, her confusion in the boss's office, only God knows what else. Beth would not be surprised to see a message from him, but was when she saw 5, coming within half an hour from each other.

"Now he'll think that I'm ignoring him."

Beth opened the messages and read one after another:

"Beth, can we talk?"

"Please let me know when we can..."

"Are you angry with me?"

"Beth, are you ok?"

"BETH please answer!"

She slowly typed:

"Sorry, I was busy."

That didn't sound like her and she knew it. She never lost touch with her phone.

Next message showed up immediately:

"I was worried. Can we talk?"

Beth just blankly stared at the screen.

"Please Beth."

Beth didn't reply.

"I'm an idiot, Beth."

She replied:

"I agree."

She felt frustration building up. He was touching the part of her soul which was confused and irritated with him. Part, which had questions, but never received answers.

He didn't answer. She continued:

"What do you want from me?"

That was harsh and Beth felt it when she pushed the send button.

"I want US."

Beth smiled. That's what he wanted.

"I want many things..."

That was a lie. She didn't. Beth always had a hard time recording herself wanting something, imagining the future, making a bucket list. Normally she didn't realize what she wanted until she was in direct contact with it. Even in clothing shops. She never came there looking for something specific. She was just browsing, touching the surfaces until the thing she liked stuck in her mind. If she didn't buy it and walked away, these things would haunt her.

But Beth technically didn't want many things. But this was a lie which sounded good in this case.

"I need to explain myself."

"You did, while sitting drunk on my couch."

"I need to explain why I left."

"I know why you left."

For a moment Beth realized that she actually did. Sober Karl was not able to keep up with the actions of the drunk one. It was a mild case of split personality. Beth laughed. How ironic was it?

"So what are we going to do about it?"

He was not apologizing anymore. Something shifted and Beth sensed it. She was intrigued and wanted to play this game.

"What do you want to do about it?"

Silence... Beth smiled. Now it was a good time for him to understand the situation for himself.

Beth was going to put a phone on the side, not expecting for anything interesting to come, when a new message popped up.

"I want to start all over again. Will you go on a date with me?"

She couldn't believe her eyes. She didn't believe her fingers when they typed and sent:

"Yes."

"Are you free on Saturday for dinner?"

"I am." Beth typed again without realizing it.

"I will pick you up at 7."

Beth just sat for a few minutes, staring at the screen, slowly realizing what she had just done.

"I guess I'm a mistress now." She said to herself and looked at the opened notebook. Sad feelings drowned her, covering up the excitement. "Not like this life will last long."

Probably they messed it up already. So what could change from going on a date with her married senior? How big is it compared with Any probably busting their cover?

Any

Any opened the notebook. First thing she noticed were traces of missing pages. That didn't happen before. She started reading. It was bad and she knew it.

"Oh Beth..." She said, touching the edges of the pages which were ripped off. "I did it again, didn't I?"

Beth is going wild now, ripping pages and going out with Karl because of her. What were the chances that the stranger will start working with Beth or even just randomly meet her? She was so careful about it and now they're in trouble again. Poor Beth...

"There should be a way..." Any thought. "I can still make it right..."

She jumped from the bed and found her phone, digging in the bunch of clothes.

There was only one message, sent same day Beth and he met:

"It might be rainy today."

It was so sweet that Any couldn't stop the radiant smile from appearing on her face.

She started typing:

"Not interesting enough."

He messaged back almost immediately:

"Skydiving?"

"Better."

"What are you up to Gingerhead? Share with me."

"I want to see the ocean."

"Road trip it is. I'll drive."

"Of course you will." Any thought. She had zero understanding of how to drive and never bothered to learn.

"12pm at the Pizza place." She texted.

"Will be there."

She was late. Bus took too long in traffic. By the time she reached the place it was almost 12.30. Any looked around. Parking was full with cars, but there were no visible humans. She walked around for a few minutes until something caught her eye. Black car, big and shiny, was parked on one side of the pizzeria. Glass was heavily toned, so she didn't see if anyone was inside. But something orange was attached to the passenger seat door. Any took a few steps further, magnetized with the beautiful colors like a fly with a light. It was a ribbon, knitted out of thin autumn colored yarn.

Any was so close to it that it would not be appropriate if she was wrong about the car. But she wasn't. Stranger opened a passenger door for her and looked straight in her glowing eyes.

"I knew you'd notice it."

"It's beautiful..."

Any unstuck the ribbon from the car door, not bothering if she scratched the car surface.

"And unique. I had it custom made for you." He was very proud of himself.

"Show off." She exclaimed, teasingly.

"It's not easy to impress my Weirdo."

That sounded off. Any immediately stopped smiling, color disappeared from her cheeks. No one ever called her "my" and it sounded shocking and oddly satisfying at the same time.

He noticed it, but didn't say anything, giving her time and space to absorb it, pretending that he was busy with getting out of overcrowded parking.

When Any was able to talk again, she highlighted with a tone of disappointed teacher: "I don't belong to you! This Weirdo is on her own!"

He smiled with an evil smile, just looking at her with his silver eyes. They both knew it was not true anymore.

They drove in silence. It was not awkward. Any thought that he was the first person in her life, who she wasn't required to talk to. They just sat in his car, listening to music in the background, staring at the road opening in front of them. She didn't want to fill the silence, she was not scared of silence probably for the first time in her life.

She jumped in her seat when she felt his ice cold hand touching hers. Her hands were hot and sweaty, as always. He took his hand away immediately, feeling her confusion.

"Just checking." He said and confused impression ran through his face.

"And you're calling me a Weirdo."

"You are. The weirdest Weirdo ever."

"Oh, sorry for pulling you out of your normal life routine!"

Any smiled straight to his face, he could count teeth in her mouth if he wanted. This smile was so different from the other one.

"I'm not the only one who has a routine..."

Evil smile appeared in the corner of his mouth again.

Any froze for a moment, looking at it.

"Who doesn't?" She said as casually as her pumping heart allowed her to do.

"You're a good actress. I believed you when you played your part in the office. I almost bought it."

Any just stared at him, feeling how her mouth is slowly drying out. He continued talking, looking at the road, not paying attention to her confused look.

"Almost bought it." He repeated.

Any realized that whatever she says now can be damaging, so she kept listening.

"You have a scar behind your left ear, it looks like a small bug. I saw it when you pulled your hair together while slicing that pizza in a park. And then I saw it again when Karl was saying something and you turned your face to him. It was there. You almost tricked me, I believed it right until the moment I saw it. There is no fucking way that two different people had the same scar. So nicely played, Beth..."

Any turned around and looked at the passenger window. Trees and houses were flashing away. He was speeding, but she didn't feel it until now.

"You lied to me." He said squeezing the wheel with both hands, not looking at her, just blankly staring at the road.

"Did I?" Any said it so quiet and distant that it sounded like it was not her at all.

He turned around and looked into her face.

She continued talking at this pace, with a trace of sadness in her voice. He stopped his car abruptly, sliding from the highway. Any felt the belt piercing in her shoulder even through her coat. He looked straight in her eyes. Volcanic orange cracks were so bright now.

"Did I?" Any repeated again. She put her hot hand on his ice cold. "Why did you touch my hand then?"

He didn't look angry anymore, confusion took over.

"I will tell you why..." Any continued. Her voice was so powerful, almost hypnotizing. She squeezed his hand in hers, covering it with her warmth.

"Your hands are hot." He said as confused as he could be. "They were hot the day we met, every time except the day you were in my office."

Any took her hand away, wanted to, but he caught it back with both his palms.

"I don't understand..." He mumbled.

"I don't ask you too. I need to fix it though." Any smiled with the corner of her mouth. "Before Beth decides to run away again."

Any pulled an orange bracelet with her other hand from under his sleeve. They both looked at it.

"You know when I'm lying, don't you?" Any sight.

He nodded.

"Am I lying when I'm saying that I've never been to your office and never met you there?"

"No." He said with growing confusion.

Any smiled, sadly this time. She looked at the window again, pulling her hands away from his. He allowed it. Suddenly he opened his door and stepped away, walked around the car, opened her door.

"Going to leave me here?" Any said laughing.

He didn't reply, just spread his hand. Any took it, and jumped out of the car. They stood next to each other in the middle of nowhere, with no visible traces of people around. Any's hair was flying all over, being played with the wind. He slowly moved closer to her, his lips almost touching her ear and whispered: "Forgive me my lady."

She didn't say a word. Her skin was burning. He stood on one knee and kissed her hand.

"I will. But you need to stop calling me Beth."

"Easy, Gingerhead!"

He jumped back on his feet and squeezed Any in his arms. She had no chance to react. They just stood like this, her face on his chest.

"And..." Any whispered to his chest: "Stop thinking that Beth is me..."

He hugged her even tighter. He didn't understand, didn't want to. Not now, not yet.

"I promise." He whispered in her ear. "I will do anything you ask."

"Show off." She whispered with a smile, hiding her face on his chest.

She never realized when it happened, but now she wanted to be his.

"I need one more thing from you." Any said standing at a jetty, watching the endless ocean tickling it with the waves. He was standing behind her, his hands wrapped around her waist.

"Anything." He said quietly.

"I want you to talk to Beth. Tomorrow, yes, as soon as you can. Go to her office, or invite her to yours. Doesn't matter. You need to convince her that she's safe... That we don't need to start over. That you will not cause issues... You need to convince her that she can continue living her life." She said it so emotionally, almost choking.

He didn't ask for an explanation, just kissed the back of her head and whispered: "I will."

"It might work." Any nodded, calming down now. She smiled for the first time in hours.

Beth

Beth was sitting in her office, hugging herself with her hands. She didn't feel like working. Computer screen went on sleeping mode a long time ago. She was brainstorming when Les broke the silence:

"What are you doing, girl?"

"Nothing." Beth shook off a serious look and smiled to a face in a doorway.

"Good, because HE wants to see you."

"Can you be more specific?"

"New boss. He asked for you. Without Karl this time. It's the first time he asked for someone. Congratulations, you're the main gossip of the day!"

"Wow! Lucky me!" Beth exclaimed sarcastically.

"He's cute, I can get it. Weird style though. Nothing that a smart woman can't correct though." Les said, fixing her shirt color while looking into a mirror.

"Don't tell me you're going to try your luck with him." Beth couldn't hold a short laugh.

"Why? Do you know something I don't?"

"Noone knows more than you in this office." Beth said with a calming voice.

Less smiled with her charming smile.

"Come in." He said when Beth knocked in the glass door.

She pulled all her internal strength to look cool and professional. He waited until she sat in a comfy chair and started talking:

"I promised to tell you something... I promised to convince you that you will be safe. I promised to convince you not to run away. There were many things I promised yesterday."

Beth felt tension building up in her body. She didn't say anything, just waited, looking into the pale gray eyes.

"But..." He continued, looking straight in her charcoal color eyes. "I just want to let you know that I will never do anything to harm you."

"I don't understand..." Beth tried to squeeze words in between his speech, but he stopped her with a tensed gesture of a pale hand and continued:

"Please don't take her away from me."

Beth scratched the armchair handle with her nails, so hard she was holding it.

"She told you..." Beth said, almost whispering.

"No." He said louder than she expected. "I... have no idea how it works. I just know what I need to... That you are not her. And that I should never call her Beth." He smiled and sudden brightness appeared on his pale face. His eyes filled with light for just a moment. He rubbed his neck showing that he still was not comfortable regarding his effort to confront Any.

Beth released the chair handle, tension was gone. She knew how annoyed Any was being called Beth.

"She hates it..." Beth nodded.

"I wanted to show you something." He pulled the phone from his pocket.

Beth was holding her breath. He turned the screen around, so she could see it and pressed a play button. Video started playing. It was Any, laying in the sand, making an angel with her stretched hands and legs.

His voice was announcing behind the camera: "You're such a Weirdo, Gingerhead!" He was laughing which Beth could hardly attach to the image of him in front of her.

Any was giggling, all her clothes and hair was covered with sand. Now Beth understood why most of the apartment looked like a beach in the morning. Suddenly the camera started falling with the person holding it. He felt in the sand right next to Any, his black hair covering her cheek. She laughed louder. Now he was filming both of them.

Beth couldn't hold her smile.

"Oh, Any..." She whispered.

He looked at her with an expression of a man who saw a lightning strike nearby.

"Any." He repeated.

Beth looked more serious now, realizing what she just did.

"She didn't tell you, didn't she?" She asked, covering her lips with her hand.

"She didn't. How foolish of me not to ask..."

Beth shook her head, regretting spoiling the secrecy of their relationships.

"Bethany." He suddenly said, clapping his hand on the surface of the wooden table. "Beth Any..." He repeated again, separate this time.

Beth nodded.

"It was written in your file... I could guess..." He mumbled.

Beth smiled. She felt so light, not playing a part. She didn't need to lie to him. This amazing feeling absorbed her.

"It might work." She concluded, looking at the screen of his phone.

"Tell me what you need me to do."

"I need you to tell her something." Beth swallowed hard, trying to keep approaching tears. "Tell her that it is her turn."

Beth stood up from her chair, trying to run away from overwhelming emotions. She was talking very professionally and business like now: "I will start thinking through the plan..." She looked at the black screen of his phone again, like a video of Any bathing in the sand was still playing there. She froze for a moment and added, demanding: "You need an official reason for us to talk. Think of something."

"Yes, ma'am." He said teasingly, effortlessly reminding her who was in charge here.

Beth blushed for a split moment, realizing in what position he was here.

"Beth." He said softly. "It will work."

She nodded.

It was a date day. Beth was sitting on the edge of her bed with her shoes on, ready to step out the moment Karl arrived.

She didn't know what to expect, so she picked out the most casual outfit she could. Her hair was pulled in a tight ponytail, but she gave it some freedom this time, so messy curls were spread all over her back. She looked different.

It was a date and she was worried. She measured the apartment in steps many times already, opened and closed her drawer just to make sure that she selected the best clothing option. Opened Any's drawer just to make sure that it is still messy. Took her time to put back stuff, which fell off it. It took minutes.

Karl was there exactly at 7, texting: "Are you ready?"

She was and he knew it without asking. Beth was never late. Even worse, most of the time she was awkwardly early. He knew it.

Beth walked down the stairs as fast as she could, considering the height of her hills. She gasped for air when she saw him standing in front of his car with a dark red rose in his hand. He smiled, seeing her shock.

"You look surprised."

"I didn't expect..."

"I'm not afraid to get caught, Beth." He said sharply.

She smiled. It was foolish, but brave. He added, buckling his belt on a driver's seat:

"Whatever happens, it's on me, not on you. It's my sin, Beth."

She wanted to argue, but didn't.

He drove, she was looking at his calm and focused face, finally breathing out:

"May I know where we are going?"

"No." He simply answered. "But soon."

Beth nodded. He stopped next to the porch of a townhouse, turned to her and said:

"I want you to meet my family."

Beth was overwhelmed so badly that she couldn't form words apart from: "What? Why? Are you crazy?"

"That's why I didn't tell you before." He admitted with a wide smile.

Beth was still gasping for air when he opened her door and gave her his hand. He almost pulled her to the front door, holding both her hand and waist.

First thing Beth saw was a round smiley face on the level of Beth's waist. It was a little girl, wearing a jeans jumpsuit. She said something in gibberish and looked at the person standing next to her. The lady looked down at a girl and smiled, saying: "Yeah, I know."

Beth was speechless.

"You must be Beth." The lady in the doorway said, stretching her hand with a wide smile.

Beth noted, automatically replying to her gesture.

"Boy your hands are cold! Come in, get comfortable."

"What the hell?" Beth whispered the moment the lady stepped back to the dining room and Karl was trying to pull Beth's coat from her shoulders.

"It's my sister." He said, not even trying to hide how much fun he was having, looking at Beth's emotions. "And my niece."

"Your family..." Beth repeated.

"The only family I've got... If not to count my wife." Karl almost choked with laughter, not expecting how comic the situation sounded.

"It's not funny." Beth whispered with the highest volume she could without anyone hearing it.

"I know." Karl said. "I'm not laughing at the situation. But you react so funny.

She slapped his chest with her palm and he caught it in his hands.

"Just bare with me." He said. "I know that it is not what you expected on the first date."

Still holding her hand, he once again pulled her shocked body to the dining room. Table was set in the middle of it, cartoons playing on the large TV, toys spread all over the floor and furniture.

Karl's sister came in from the kitchen holding another dish. She looked tired, that was the kind of tiredness you can see only in parents faces. She looked at the child, trying to climb a couch by herself to watch TV with more comfort, than she looked back at Beth. Her face was pale, her hair was blonde, the same shade as the little ponytail on the child's head.

"He didn't tell you where you were going, did he?" Karl's sister smiled.

"Does he do it often?" Beth didn't expect this sarcastic thone from herself.

She shook her head, saying: "He never did it. I just saw it on your face. Yeah, I know, a weird choice for a first date."

Beth wanted to defend herself, to say that she was not dating him, that it is all absurd, that Karl is married and can't be dating... but she just stood there in the middle of the living room, puzzled. The scenario didn't add up in her head. Karl's sister noticed her expression and pointed to one of the chairs. Child was saying something exciting in an unknown language in the background.

Beth sat on a chair, everyone joined her, except for a little one, who was absorbed into action on the TV screen.

After few awkward minutes of putting food in plates, Karl's sister started talking, with a soft storytelling thone:

"When we were kids, we had this family tradition. It was called "No judgment dinner." Every once in a while we ate dinner behind the table and had a talk. Whatever you say there would not be judged not that day, not in future. It was a good time to spill out your secrets, or speak up about mistakes you made. You'll be listened to, you'll be heard. That was it. No one would point fingers or get angry. It was extremely hard for everyone first, with years we just adjusted.

I remember calling for this dinner to announce that I started dating a guy, who was...let's say bad influence. My father almost broke rules that day, punching the table hard with his fists. My mother calmed him down in the kitchen and they returned to a table in peace, holding hands. I still remember his face when he pronounced "No judgment" with his voice broken, not looking in my eyes. I was not judged, but I couldn't stand it either. Relationships were never a success, if you ask me. It took me longer to break the silence I received from my parents. Silence is worse than judgment, trust me. I couldn't bear it."

She sipped water from a glass in front of her, through a glance at a child, singing something in the background and came back to her story.

"I don't know if it was right or wrong. We just had it and this tradition made us more understanding and patient to each other. We could talk about everything..."

She took one more sip, it was obvious that the story was getting harder for her to tell with each word. Beth was all ears.

"...When we lost our parents, there were no dinners anymore. Life through us apart, we dealt with it separately. For years we barely even met or talked. We were like the only witnesses of each other's pain. I was trying to be more like his mother, than sister. I was older than him, it was my duty to take care of him. He didn't take it well though. We grew apart even more. One day despite every common sense I just picked up the phone and called for a "no judgment dinner". He was there. We sat behind this table, the same table we sat with our parents and talked. I told him that I'm pregnant, that I will marry a guy and try to build a family with him. I didn't have a good job, neither did he, no savings, no plan. The look on Karl's face was exactly the same as the look on the face of our father when I was 16. I remember how he barely audibly pronounced "no judgment" and we moved on. It was what I needed then. The father of my child didn't last long, our marriage fell apart within months. I called Karl again that day, and we talked again. It was easier this time. Slowly we recovered a tradition and became more involved in each other's lives. It was mostly me, calling for these dinners though. Yeah, I know, that I'm a mess. Few weeks ago was the first time Karl called for it. I was intrigued. What did he want to confess? Everything looked so stable and controlled in his life, especially compared to mine."

She looked around with an ironic smile.

"He came here and we sat behind the table. How surprised I was to hear that his life is way less perfect than I expected. We drank a lot that day. It was tough. He told me about you. He explained to me of this unbearable internal fight he's having every single time he sees you. I remember how I smiled, realizing that he's also a human, that he's tempted and messed up. He talked a lot about you, I listened. I didn't even think of judging him. The story touched my soul. Last week he called me to tell how he opened up to you, how he ran away, scared to listen to your side of the story. I offered him to invite you here. I'm happy to welcome you here, Beth, on our "No judgment dinner."

Beth didn't know what to say. She just looked at Karl, who now had a mild blush on his cheeks.

"I'm honored to be here. I think that's exactly what I needed today... On my first date with a married guy."

"No judgment, dear." Karl's sister said softly with a wide smile.

The child suddenly slided from a couch and ran to her mother, clearly pronouncing "Mama!", but everything else was a very clear gibberish. Karl's sister pulled a girl up, to sit on her knees and listened carefully to everything that small one had to say. She replied, softly, kissing her pink cheek: "I have no idea what you are trying to tell me, but one day I will understand you."

It was so heartwarming that Beth almost broke into tears.

When dinner was over, Beth and Karl were sitting in his car again, silent. Beth looked at the porch of this house which felt so much as home.

"Thank you." She said, "For bringing me here. It was a great first date."

"And now we're back to a dangerous world, where everyone is against us." He said with a wide ironic smile.

"Can we stay out of this world for a little longer?"

"What's on your mind?"

Beth smiled and looked in his eyes. She saw something she never saw before. He was relaxed and looked completely happy.

"I just want to remember it." She said, touching his cheek with the tips of her fingers.

He suddenly said something she heard earlier this week from another man. Exactly the same: "Beth... It will work."

She nodded, hiding how surprised she was with this deja vu.

Any

"I can't believe that it's actually real." He was standing in a bedroom, looking at two sides of a huge clothing cabinet, one side filled with neat clothes mostly in dark colors, the other - overloaded with clothes of all possible colors, but mainly orange.

"I can't believe that you're in my bedroom." Any said smiling, with mild blush all over her cheeks. She never opened Beth's part of the cabinet before, considering it an invasion of her privacy.

He just stood there, looking at their two lives, squeezed in one cabinet.

"How long are you doing it?" He asked with the sad thone in his voice.

"That's what you want to know?" Any giggled. She didn't expect this question. She added quietly: "For as long as I remember. It was not that clear in the beginning, we didn't notice. There was no clear line. Just headaches and blackouts... It took us time to understand what was happening. It took us way longer to understand how to make it work."

"What about your parents?"

"Oh, them. When we were small, they just thought that it was a well developed imagination, then for a short time they considered that we were sick... Doctors, hospitals, tests.

Thankfully, Beth was already smart enough to understand that it's better to hide it after all. Then they were too busy to notice... and Beth was already very skilled with developing strategies. Now, we live far from them and barely talk or see each other. Better, easier this way."

He felt a hidden bitterness of this story.

"Do you miss them?" He said, assuming that this was causing her sadness.

"Not really." She replied blankly, staring at the window. "I was never part of a picture. They have only one daughter and I'm not her."

"Did you try to tell them the truth?" He asked, realizing that he was scratching her old, barely healed wound.

She shook her head.

There was a line he couldn't cross. Not now, not yet.

"Too painful." He made a mental note to himself.

Before he was able to recover, to change a subject or at least to make her smile again, they heard someone knocking in the door.

The expression on Any's face was worthy of an Oscar nomination. It changed from slightly sad to surprised and then to extremely excited in a split second.

"Hide!" She whispered with her widest smile, barely holding herself from laughing in his face.

The idea of hiding a guy in her bedroom was so exciting, she couldn't resist. Most probably it was not even necessary, but she still wanted to do it. Just to tick one more goal in her list... maybe to add it to the list first and then scratch it out.

He was standing in the middle of her bedroom, barely believing that probably he will actually need to hide any time soon.

"Just kidding." Any said, holding an approaching laugh with her palm, almost choking with it, seeing his confused expression. It was very slight though. From outside he always looked cold and distant, she learned to read these light traces of emotions in his eyes and she felt that no one else could do it. Without realizing it, he opened up to her. It was more than she could ask for. It was bigger than anything he felt to another human being. Trust. He trusted her enough to take away his guard for a split second from time to time.

"Two visitors in one day." She whispered with the playful twinkle in her eyes. "Lucky me!"

Any closed the bedroom door, not breaking eye contact with him, standing in the same spot.

"Trev!" She exclaimed probably too loud while seeing his smiling face in the doorway.

"Beth!" He did the same.

Any smiled even wider, trying to hide the cringes she caught from it. Trev smiled back. Weird feelings rushed through his body.

"We're meeting again. I mean neighbors meeting. On Sunday. I don't know if anyone told you. Kat said that she didn't catch you and she left a note."

"Note." Any looked around automatically. "I didn't see it." She admitted.

"That's what I thought." Trev exclaimed happily, realizing that he did the right thing. He didn't want to be invasive and now he officially wasn't. That added more confidence.

"Sunday." Any repeated. "I need to check my work schedule. I hope I can make it! It was so fun last time!" For a split second, she thought how interesting this situation was. She was talking about Beth's schedule and behind her bedroom door was a man who was powerful enough not only to adjust Beth's schedule, but to terminate her employment.

Trev ended the conversation soon, for it not to become awkward. Going down the stairs he slightly moved his head, trying to shake away the weird feeling. He could swear that the Beth who opened the door now and the one who did it last time were two different people. He knew how ridiculous and impossible it sounded, but it was there. This feeling has stalked him for a while now. It started when he took a sketchbook in his hands, feeling inspiration to draw Beth's portrait. He remembered an internal voice asking him which one he wanted to draw. That was weird. It was the same feeling now, asking "Which one do you want to see?" He shook it away, like he did before.

"I'm getting crazy..." He mumbled to himself on his way downstairs.

"Did I tell you that Beth and I are working really hard on a new plan?" He said looking at Any's feet, covered with bright colored socks. They were sitting on her couch, watching a movie. Her feet were on his knees, huge bowl of popcorn in her hands, bucket size drink on the coffee table. He couldn't stop staring at her feet, she moved them without realizing while something exciting was happening on the screen. It reminded him of a purring cat, softly spreading and tightening back tiny paws. It was obvious that Any was not doing it intentionally as she was absorbed in the movie action. He was watching the movie, but her subtle toe movements were so relaxing that he couldn't distract himself from it.

"How is it going?" Any replied blankly, putting the next popcorn piece in her mouth, not breaking eye contact with the TV screen.

He released a deep sight.

"Contain the issue, investigate, create a plan, act... or something like that." Any recited with the same blank expression. "Do you actually think that it's the first time she's trying to keep me away from the outside world?" Any looked at him now with a sad twinkle in her eyes.

He didn't reply, realizing that Beth actually tricked him into the idea to reduce public appearance with Any, to spend some time with her at home, watching movies.

She knew. He forgot that Any was dealing with Beth all her life and could predict her reactions.

"Now you know." Any giggled, looking at his puzzled face.

"I..." He started saying.

"No worries, I know you didn't mean it. Beth can be very convincing regarding safety measures. And now she will be extra proactive because she never wanted to stay that badly. She needs it to work. A lot of pressure..."

"How long does it normally take before you...change location?"

Any released short laugh, popcorn piece almost flew out of her mouth before she managed to stop it with her palm.

"Depending on how close we grow with people around. The closer and faster we do it, the earlier we need to go."

"Did you ever grow so close?" He asked, moving closer to her, forcing her into a hug.

"Not really..." Any bit her thumb, thinking.

He smiled. That was sincere.

"She is trying hard to figure it out this time." He said.

"Of course she does." Any thought. She knew something he didn't. Beth was not only trying to make Any's life a success. She had something worth staying for also, someone she wanted to be with.

Beth

"Did you hear what happened?" Les appeared in Beth's office earlier than expected. Beth barely had time to hang her coat and was startled with it. Normally Les gave her a chance to switch on her computer. Matter was clearly urgent.

"I knew something was wrong with him." Les made her regular stop next to Beth's mirror, checking if her hairstyle still was perfect.

"I need more details." Beth declared, putting her bag on the table and following her regular routine.

"Why did you come so late today by the way? You missed everything."

Beth yawned and smiled.

"Late night adventures." Truthfully Beth had no idea why it was impossible for her to open her eyes early today. She woke up drained. Maybe it was a late night, but not hers.

"I didn't know that you have a double life." Les sent a killing spark with her eyes in Beth's direction. It hurted Beth straight in her chest, making it harder to process air. She had no idea how close it was to reality. Beth forced an ironic smile, breathing out with the last air she had left:

"I didn't know you lost your sense of humor."

Les laughed almost hysterically, Beth watched her ponytail moving from one shoulder to another.

"Sorry, I completely forgot that you are an incurable workaholic and a terrible old lady who forgot how it is actually to have fun at night."

Beth finally restored her ability to breathe. Panic attack was not approaching anymore. Danger was not anywhere near her now.

"That's all me..." Beth pretended to focus on the filling of her bag, thinking what she will need to use during her day today. It was impossible to focus, her mind was blurry.

"Don't you tell me that you're not curious at all!"

"Regarding what?" Beth dropped herself into a chair, realizing that she completely forgot to pretend to be interested in whatever happened in the office before she came. She looked at Les, who was mildly disappointed.

"Are you feeling ok?" The only explanation Les could think of was that Beth was not feeling well, that is why she was not immediately curious regarding her news.

"I had better mornings." Beth mumbled, touching her forehead with ice cold, but sweaty hand. She was wondering now if her glasses got foggy, or if it was one of the symptoms of whatever she experienced today.

"Morning? It's 11.30am. Oh, God, Beth. You're not well at all! Please don't tell me that I need to call an ambulance again today. Twice in a row!"

"Ambulance?" Beth was stunned with this word. She finally started to put together why Les was on the nerves since she came in today. "What happened?" She exclaimed.

"Your boss..." Less made a dramatic pause, just to see if Beth is shocked enough to lose it, to spill out something Les can use later for her deductions. She knew that something was definitely going on between Beth and Karl, also she had weird feelings about her and new boss. It was not fitting in her mind that Beth was fooling around with both of them, so she made an effort to investigate further and to deduce, which one of these two different men was actually Beth's lover. But there was no evidence! All of them were extremely professional, especially in her presence. Now was her chance to figure it out. Yes, it was cruel to watch Beth reacting, but this was currently the only way to catch her off guard. That is why Les was not saying any names...yet.

Beth's eyes became so big, energy was now flowing out of them. Les even thought that she noticed orange cracks in her black eyes for a split moment, but later assumed that it was just a lighting change. Beth's cheeks were burning with a feverish blush. She stood up from her chair so fast that she needed to use her hands to stabilize herself and use all her strength to fight the nauseous feeling.

"Karl?" She whispered, realizing that her cold fingers were too sweaty now and were sliding on the table. She looked Les straight in the eyes, understanding what she was doing, realizing that Les was watching her as a hawk now, but not caring. If something happened to Karl, she didn't care if Les would assume that there's something more between them.

Les found what she was looking for. Beth was definitely more worried now than a normal person would be if she heard something like this about her boss. Deep inside she was applauding her wonderful deductive skills and for an ability to read people this way. She got what she wanted, now there was no reason to torture this poor lover.

"No, another one." Les announced and added, seeing Beth's reaction. "The fresh addition to the team."

Moment ago Les thought that she had Beth in her fist, knowing everything she needed about her hidden life, but now something different was happening. Beth's face was projecting emotions which Les never saw and definitely didn't expect to see now. First, she was obviously relieved that the story was not about Karl. Second, her energy shifted. For a split second Les thought that her eyes turned fiery orange again, her hair became brighter and her posture was so strong and confident like never before. But it was only for a second and Les just couldn't find another explanation to it that sudden light from the bright window. Beth was obviously worried, maybe even more than she was for a moment she assumed it was Karl.

Les was puzzled now. Maybe her deduction skills were not that brilliant after all. But this time it was not a mild look of a worried lover, it was a wild look of an animal looking in the eyes of danger. Les was amazed, not realizing that Beth was even capable of this kind of emotion. She was watching this shift without blinking, trying to understand it. She was watching wild Beth calming herself down now, she was not "glowing" anymore, emotions were back under control.

"What happened?" She whispered, looking at Les, looking tired from all the spectrum of emotions she experienced for the last few minutes. She was definitely not feeling well, or even not being fully herself today.

Les was not able to comprehend it, not now at least. So she started the story, still watching Beth, but realizing that the moment had passed and now she will not project anything curious:

"I don't actually know. Paramedics are not much of talkers. And I was busy, holding the crowd away from him and calling his father... That was one hell of a morning."

"What do you know?" Beth asked with perfect understanding that Les knew way much more than she wanted to show.

"I saw him fainting." Les concluded with such a cold tone which she could use for reciting her daily to do list. "I was passing by the glass door of his office at the right moment. He was just standing next to the window one second and the next one he was on the floor. Thank God that carpet is so soft, he could hurt himself."

Beth was not breathing. It was not a panic attack this time, she was just scared to breathe, so she will not be able to hear Les.

"I called an ambulance." Les said with a lifeless thone. "They took him to the hospital. What I know for sure, he was definitely breathing when they were loading him in the car."

Beth exhaled for the first time, realizing that she was choking herself and breathing in as slow as she could.

"Which hospital?"

That was a question Les didn't expect. She could not believe it. Beth was involved in a relationship with him? Why else would she care so much? No one else in the office was asking her where the new boss was taken to give him a visit. She shook her head, grieving on her unsuccessful attempt to read Beth's reactions and to identify her romantic interest. Now she was even more confused.

"St. Michael's." Les said, watching Beth taking her wallet from a bag and putting on her coat. "What are you doing?"

"I'm going there." Beth acted intuitively, her mind was too blurry to analyze and plan. She felt how her body was performing movements, but had very little control of it.

Les just stood frozen, watching Beth leaving.

"Are you serious?" She mumbled when Beth was next to the elevator, pressing the button.

Beth just ignored it. It was not important. The only thing she was thinking about was to get to a hospital in one piece. She didn't want to drive. Not now. She stepped on a street, feeling cold air streaming to her face, refreshing, almost freezing.

Taxi took a long time in traffic. Minutes lasted as hours. Beth was blankly staring at the window, squeezing and releasing the bottom of her jacket, using it as the banana shaped antistress tool she had in her office. It helped, but not that much. She realized how stupid it was just to take off, go to a hospital, just to find out if he is ok. Since she heard the news, he became the most precious person in her life, she was ready to give up everything just to know that he is still breathing. That's what Les said. He was breathing. Not much of the details.

Beth was briefly remembering the details of her first aid training which she took years ago just for general knowledge. During these few days she learned a lot not only about saving lives. She learned something about herself, she knew now that she would never be able to save anyone, even if she knew all the theory and practiced all the actions on the manikin. It seemed easy, there was a set of actions that she needed to perform, one after another. She could do it with her eyes closed. She actually did it once, witnessing an old man falling in the middle of the park, while he was reading a book on the bench. She did everything right, according to a plan. Paramedic said that she did a good job, maybe even saved an old man's life. She did well, that's what they said. But Beth knew something about herself they didn't. She was not able to perform this way if something like this would happen to someone she cared about. Knowing all the theory and practicing was not enough. If something happened to a person who was close to her heart, she would just freeze and be the most useless person ever.

Taxi driver was picking on her in the mirror. The way she intensely stared at the window without seeing anything in front of her was bothering him.

"Are you ok, miss?" He asked, looking at the mirror, hoping that she would wake up now from this emotionless state.

Beth turned her head in his direction so fast that he almost jumped in his seat.

"I'm…" She mumbled, feeling how dry her mouth was. She cleared her throat. "Hospital…" She said, understanding that she was not saying anything new to him. She added, trying to clarify the situation: "They took him to the hospital. He was breathing." That didn't make any sense, but that was the only thought she had now.

She remembered the first aid instructor saying something like: "If the person is breathing, the situation is not that bad. You have a chance to call an ambulance." Breathing was a good sign, that's what she knew. It was the only useful detail apart from the hospital's name that Les shared. She knew that Les was using this case to read her, she knew that she might just put herself in big trouble. She didn't care.

Taxi driver shook his head, slowly pronouncing, giving her confused brain to absorb the meaning of his words: "Don't worry miss, we're almost there."

Beth stared at the window again, seeing a line up of ambulance cars a walking distance from them. She nodded, still staring at the window. The only thing she could see now was a huge hospital building and people moving in and out, like bees in a hive.

Reception was empty, few nurses were sitting behind a glass, focusing on the screens in front of them. Beth approached one of them, trying to put the words in the correct order, to clear her blurry mind and to listen as sharp as it was possible to all the information the nurse will be able to share. She was piercing her palms with her fingernails so hard that one of two things was going to happen: or her nails would be broken, or her skin would start bleeding.

Nurse was looking at her with a soft smile and mild concern. According to her experience, the best thing she could do now, was to let Beth see this man and to convince her that nothing is threatening his life anymore, or she will have one more patient in her hands. Beth was definitely not feeling well. Beth was literally suffocating her with the emotions she was experiencing. Nurse looked at her screen again, feeling how Beth was staring at her without blinking. Nurse looked back at the pale face, framed with a dark ginger hair and exhaled:

"Maam... Just follow the blue line on the floor until it guides you to room 110."

Beth nodded and looked at the floor. Thankfully, her mind was clear enough to differentiate colored lines on the floor. She started moving slowly, then faster, gaining confidence. It was not far, it barely took her a few minutes to reach the right door. That was a moment when her mind went blank again. She didn't even think of knocking, just turned the handle and entered the room. First thing she saw was sunlight caught in the curtains hanging over the huge window. Room was blindingly bright with its white walls and furniture. That was how Beth imagined heaven.

He was standing in between a big white hospital bed and a bunch of screens and monitors. He was wearing black trousers and holding black shirt in his hand, probably planning to put it on. Beth noticed how pale his skin was, especially in this bright light and compared to a black clothes. His eyes looked pale and lifeless, with gray circles under them. He was also skinnier than she imagined him to be. Now she clearly saw that there was zero fat between his skin and muscles. He looked fit and unhealthy at the same time.

For a few seconds Beth was just standing in a doorway, staring at his naked torso, feeling life and color coming back to her cheeks as they started burning. Now when she saw him standing, her mind started working clearly again, figuring out what to do next.

He was looking at her with mixed feelings. Finally he broke the silence:

"Knocking would be nice." He started pulling his left hand through the shirt sleeve.

Beth felt her face burning. She was standing here in front of her half naked boss and was finally realizing how stupid she was to assume all these horrible things happening to him. He looked alive and well now.

"Calling would be better!" She exclaimed with more irritation than she expected from herself.

He measured her with a devilish smile and twinkle in his pale eyes: "Don't tell me you were worried."

Beth felt ridiculous, but was not ready to give up now, after all the stupid things she did already, probably ruining everything she was building for months.

"I came as soon as i found out."

"You shouldn't."

"I know..." Beth looked at her feet. "I didn't think straight. I just couldn't."

"Sorry for that. I was sort of relieved that you were not in the office when it happened."

"What happened?" Beth whispered, realizing that overwhelming emotions are blocking her voice from sounding normal now.

"Nothing much. Just a routine visit to a hospital."

"In an ambulance?"

"Happens..."

"Really?" Beth sensed building frustration in her voice.

"Good as new now!" He said, smiling with a corner of his mouth.

Beth looked at his hands. He was struggling to button up his shirt, his hands were shaking.

"I see." She said, stepping forward, not breaking eye contact with his fingers.

He looked at her surprised, not understanding what her plan was. She was standing in a hand reach of him, looking and sounding more confident now, more like Beth.

"I need to know what happened." She said,

"No, you don't." He said, looking at her with the mysterious look of a magician, who is not ready to open his secrets.

"I..." Beth started, but he interrupted.

"No. But you need to promise me something."

"What?"

"Don't tell her... please. I don't want her to know. Yet, maybe ever... I Haven't decided yet."

"Why?"

"So she will not look at me like you're looking now."

These words echoed in Beth's mind. She was sitting in her bed this evening, with her notebook on her knees and a pen in between her fingers.

"Struggle is real." She thought. For a few minutes now she was sitting like this, trying to finalize one small decision. Should she tell Any about it? Should she warn her? Will it scare her? Will she overreact? Is it even Beth's business to get involved?

Beth rubbed her forehead. Too complicated...

Deep inside she understood that this decision is not something she should be worried about. What was more scary now is her feelings. Once again she was replaying in her head her actions between conversation with Les and her boss in a hospital. It was so out of character for her to behave this way, to lose it this way. She kept replaying in her mind the conversation with Karl on the phone after the hospital. She didn't want to come back to the office, she told him that she didn't feel like herself today. That was true and it was terrifying.

"Do you want me to come over?" He asked, she felt a genuine concern in his voice.

"No..." She answered. "I just want to be alone tonight. It was a very weird day."

He understood, he received the message she was trying to send. At least one of them understood.

Beth, once again, put aside her notebook, rubbing her temple. Pain was almost unbearable.

She heard someone knocking at the front door and looked at the bedside clock. It was almost 11pm. She had no idea who that could be. She never had late visitors before.

"Maybe the delivery guy is just confused with the apartment number." Beth thought as it was the only reasonable explanation.

She slid from under the blanket in her pajama and went to a front door, opening it without hesitation.

First thing she felt was a fresh cold air on her face and bare feet. Second was a surprise. Last person who she expected to see in her doorway was a man wearing a long black coat. Beth breathed in cold air so deep inside her lunges that it started feeling cold inside also. He was standing in her doorway holding a flower, one huge red rose on the long leg. For a moment Beth thought that she just fell asleep and it was a dream, so surreal it felt.

He was looking at her for a moment, his eyes went through all the details: messy bedtime hair, gray striped pajamas, bare feet. He noticed everything and Beth felt like he just scanned her all the way through, sort of like an MRI machine.

"I came bearing gifts..." He said with his cold low voice, which was echoing through Beth's soul more than a cold night air.

He put his left wrist up and Beth saw that he was holding a bag of takeout food in it. Without saying a word, she just opened the door wider, letting him in, following him to her own kitchen.

While he was putting takeout boxes out of the bag on her kitchen table, she finally said:

"This is so inappropriate..."

"Do you think so?" He said, still looking at the content of the bag.

"I sure do... You shouldn't be here."

"Well, I was not thinking straight." His pale eyes struck her straight to her soul. It was something she told him today, it was her poor excuse of coming to see him in a hospital. Beth swallowed it.

"I'm not the one you need to see right now..." Beth was not giving up.

"Are you the one I really want to see now? Not really... Are you the one that I need to apologize to? I guess so..."

"Apologize?"

"You did something nice today. Actually you did something way out of your character... It may sound silly, but I just felt like you needed someone to talk to after you screwed up so badly. I know I might not be your first choice..."

Beth thought about how she rejected Karl earlier. He wanted to come over, to take care of her, to talk.

"I do feel awful." She whispered, rubbing her temples harshly, almost hurting herself even more.

"I am known as a good listener, I can be your stranger in a train for tonight."

He knew about it. Any always used this weird term. Beth smiled, probably for the first time today. Within an hour they were sitting on a couch, consuming delicious food he brought. It didn't feel awkward as they just talked. For the first time in years Beth was just spilling her thoughts at him. Without any filter or self control.

"It just felt off..." She whispered, holding her hands on her heart, just to make sure it would not jump out of her chest. "I don't remember half of the way to the hospital."

"People react differently in stressful conditions."

"I shouldn't react like this!" Beth suddenly exclaimed, almost dropping the box with food on the floor. "Look at Les! She was not stressed."

"For Les I'm just a new figure on a chess board, maybe a bit newer and shinier than others."

"She is not heartless, you know."

"I didn't say it." He was not even looking at her, focusing mostly on catching food from the box with chopsticks.

"I should react exactly the same as she did."

"That would be slightly disappointing."

"Yeah, much better was to embarrass myself in front of her, the whole office and you."

"That's not what happened."

"So what happened then?"

"I don't know, but I'm here to figure it out."

Suddenly, without giving a warning he touched her hand. Beth sensed it with all her body. It felt like a lightning strike. He withdrew his hand shortly. She looked at him, her face blushing, her eyes questioning his action.

"Your hand is warm." He just commented. Making a mental note of it, scratching the bottom of the take out box with his chopsticks.

Beth didn't understand. She just looked at him, realizing that he knew something she didn't.

3...2...1...

Beth opened her eyes. It was late, it felt like it. Her head was heavy, she probably overslept badly.

"Being late again. Good job, Beth!" She told herself, pulling her face away from the pillow and looking at the bedside clock.

"Why didn't I hear the alarm?" She was wondering. Beth normally was wide awake since the first sounds of it, but not today. How could she even miss it?

She tried to pull herself together, rubbing her swollen sleepy face.

"Come on Beth! What's wrong with you?"

She thought of yesterday, the day after the hospital incident. It was so awkward to step in the office and face Les, Karl, to hear barely noticeable gossips, to see the eyes following her. She just needed to survive this Friday, then Saturday was Any's and it should get easier on Sunday in the office. Fresh start of the week, normally people had a lot to share. High hopes.

Les was standing in the doorway of her office with a wide smile. She was trying to read Beth, to catch her by surprise, but she hadn't. Beth was ready this time. Impeccable look, all emotions tied up and hidden in the darkest corner of her mind.

Yesterday late night talk helped a lot, she felt easier and stronger, she was powerful enough to hold the line.

"Beth!" Les exclaimed with unrealistic excitement. "How are you feeling?"

Beth smiled with the look of an ice queen. Les looked disappointed. It was working so far. Les couldn't break through this wall and they both knew it.

"Operation successful." Beth said to herself, ticking the list in her mind next to Les name. They went to get coffee from the staff room. Beth noticed a movement in the boss's office. Only a subtle dark shadow in a bright sunny office. He was at work today. After being hospitalized yesterday, he was here. They didn't talk about it yesterday, but she knew that he will be here and he will do his best to share the office awkwardness that she was going to face.

Les didn't notice Beth thinking about it. She was talking about random office news, trying to beat Beth's guard with tricky questions. Beth knew exactly what was happening. She was herself and was able to resist now.

Completion of Karl's mission went smoothly as well. They met in his office, they talked business, they smiled. The moment Beth stepped out of his office, she received a text from him: "I'm happy you feel better today. I missed you."

He said he wanted to meet on Saturday. Beth bit her lip. Now she needed to lie. One of the reasons why Beth was avoiding the relationship was lying. For a moment she was feeling jealous of Any, who managed to open up. Sort of. As far as Beth knew, Any didn't say anything, didn't explain, didn't need to.

"Lucky girl." Beth thought. "I'm nowhere near telling Karl about it..."

It was one awkward day, but Beth handled it gracefully.

Her victorious memories of yesterday were squeezed out of her head with a massive headache. This wave was so strong that Beth almost cried. The sound was not helping. It was distant, but definitely in the room. It took time for Beth to realize that it was coming from Any's closet. She climbed out of bed, trying not to move her head much and not to cause more pain. It was Any's phone and it barely ever rang before. Beth saw message notifications and even without opening them she knew that it was from him. But getting messages here was not what struck Beth, it was the date on the phone screensaver. With the bright colorful letters it was showing "Saturday". It hit her. The reason why Beth didn't hear the alarm was because it was not set. It was not Sunday as she assumed... It was not her day.

Beth closed her eyes, trying to think, but it was too painful. Still holding Any's phone in her hand she rushed to the kitchen to get painkillers. It worked within minutes, very long and painful minutes. Pain didn't go away completely, it was just hidden in the background now, like a wild animal hiding in a cave. But it was better, Beth could work with it now. She looked at Any's phone again. The urge to open messages was strong, but it didn't feel right.

"Where are you, Any?" Was crawling through Beth's mind. She dropped herself on a bed again, taking her phone in the other hand and typing:

"She's not here."

"Beth?"

"Yes, it's only me..."

"Should she be here today?"

Beth nodded.

"She should."

"What happened?"

"I have no idea. It never happened before. She is not here. It's only me and my massive headache."

"Do you need anything?"

Beth smiled. He was disappointed. She couldn't replace Any for him, but apparently she was the nearest he could get today. Without answering his question, she typed, apologetically:

"I don't know what happened."

Suddenly an idea popped in her bruised mind and she rushed to her notebook, opening it with a hope to clarify something, but disappointed. Nothing new was written. Beth picked up her phone and texted:

"She didn't write anything in a notebook..."

He didn't answer. He was probably trying to figure out what to do and how to spend his day without Any. Beth didn't know the details, but probably they had plans. Sometimes unique and adventurous. For a split second Beth felt jealous.

"Do you need anything?" He typed again, not letting it be unanswered.

"I'm good." Beth answered briefly.

She needed something he couldn't give her. Understanding of what happened. She closed her eyes, fighting through a numb headache.

For the rest of the day Beth didn't know what to do. From one side, she finally had a day to herself without a need to be at work. From the other side, she felt like crap. Headache was coming and going. Beth was worried that she would consume so many painkillers that she would stop feeling anything. She just ended up laying on the couch with her face covered with a wet cold towel. It helped a bit and Beth was able to put her thoughts together at least.

Any

3...2...1...

Any opened her eyes and saw a bright sunlight streaming through a living room window. She was on a couch, damp towel next to her head, surrounded with pillows and blankets. Bucket with melted ice cream was standing on the coffee table in a hand reach. That was something new. Any rushed up to reach a notebook, but felt light dizziness.

"OK, we need to slow down."

She made one more attempt and it worked this time. Beth's phone was nearby and Any was seeing that the notifications screen was full.

She started reading, slowly gaining the realization of what happened. Beth made a brief, but colorful story about her unbearable headache. But that was not the main point. Beth was terribly worried about Any, because something like this never happened before.

"I know." Any said to herself quietly. "Poor Beth." She continued, looking at the mess surrounding her. She realized that a picture like that was possible only in case Beth was struggling.

Any stood up slowly and patiently, containing her desire to run to her drawer and get her phone. She needed to act fast, according to a growing list of messages and phone calls on

Beth's phone display, but she couldn't afford falling and hurting herself. It took her a few minutes to reach the bedroom. She smiled seeing a bunch of notifications on her phone too. She opened them and a bright smile spread all over her face. He was waiting, he was worried.

Not knowing what to say, she typed:

"I'm here. Please cover Beth at work."

Response came almost immediately, like he was holding his phone in his hands waiting for the moment to send it:

"Already did. Made some stories. They brought it, Karl and Les are suspicious, but we will figure it out. No worries."

"Thank you." Any typed, feeling grateful blush on her cheeks. He got it covered. He knew they needed it and jumped in. For the first time in her life she didn't regret having a person who knew about her. He helped.

"I missed you, Gingerhead. I was worried. " He typed.

"I know. Beth had a hard time yesterday."

There was a moment of silence. Any stuck looking at the couch area, picturing Beth suffering all day. When the phone vibrated, she almost dropped it, lost in her thoughts.

"I'm wrapping up a few things at work and will be on my way."

She smiled again. He was determined. Any took a moment to form a question that was bothering her and not only her according to Beth's notes the other day.

"Do you think they suspect something about you and Beth?"

"If they were not, they are now. Maybe I shouldn't jump in and cover... I think I might make it worse. Sorry."

"You did the right thing." At least she thought so.

Any looked at Beth's phone. Without opening the messenger, she knew that most of the messages were from Karl. He was worried, probably angry and jealous. Now he realized that Beth was probably dating both of them: him and their boss. Could he judge her, being a married man? It was too complicated for Any to solve.

"I'm on my way." He texted and Any experienced a weird mix of excitement and panic. Both her and the apartment were a mess and she barely had time to sort it out. Knowing that, she still texted:

"What did you tell them?"

"That Beth decided to extend her hiking trip for one more day and the network is very poor there. They still have questions though, probably because it's not clear how I knew about it... and why am I rushing out of office now. Don't worry, we'll figure it out."

Any closed her eyes, thinking. She knew that it was one of his suggestions to Beth. When they were planning how to build their life, he offered to pretend to be in relationships. Beth didn't want to do it this way. First, it would damage her image and career, second, it would complicate her real personal life, which was already not easy. Beth didn't want it, but slowly everything was leading to it. Even without them announcing it, people talked. Any was never in that office, but she was familiar enough with human nature to understand how it was developing.

She decided to stop thinking about it, rushed into the bathroom and splashed cold water on her face. It felt so satisfying. She looked in the mirror. Her reflection was blurry, but clear enough for her to see the traces of Beth's condition yesterday. She looked tired, but her eyes were glowing and it was serving as a pretty good cover up. She was blushing, thinking about him, his messages. He missed her. It felt so nice to have someone missing her.

She rushed to the door hearing him knocking and almost slipped on her way, but managed to keep balance. Excitement was overwhelming.

She heard a phone vibrating in her hand and she pulled her hand from the door, the second she felt it. Why would he text her standing next to her door? She read the message.

"Don't open."

"Why?" She texted back.

"It's not me."

Any just stood frozen within a hand reach of the door, hearing someone knocking again.

"Who is it?" She texted.

"Karl." He answered and added: "I saw him coming up. Why is he here, any ideas?"

Any felt her face burning. It was not her secret to share, but she didn't have many options now. She quietly moved back from the door, far enough so she would not be heard.

"He and Beth... they have something going on between them." That was the softest way Any could put it.

"Are they together? That explains a lot. That's why she didn't want us to pretend...I see."

Any just stood staring at the phone screen, waiting for him to figure it out. It took him a few moments. New message came:

"I thought he's married."

Any bit her lip, slowly typing: "He is."

"Oh... I see. That's why you didn't tell me."

"Not my secret. Please don't tell Beth that I told you."

"He's leaving now." He texted.

Any took a deep breath. Within a few hours they made Beth's life so much more complicated. Now Karl was jealous and he definitely didn't believe his boss's story. It will not be easy to fix.

"It's me now." She heard him knocking softly and rushed to the door again. Within moments she was squeezed in his arms, hearing his heartbeat through the thick black coat.

"How long are we going to pretend that nothing happened yesterday?" He asked, trying to throw a peanut as close to a squirrel as he could.

They were sitting on the park bench, surrounded with ancient giant trees. Big bag of peanuts was stuffed between them, squirrels jumping from one tree to another, ignoring all the peanuts thrown their way for the last half an hour, minding their own business.

"I don't understand... Maybe these peanuts are not good?" Any said, staring at the one she was holding in her hand.

"Yeah, blame the peanuts..." He dropped sarcastically. It was obvious now that he was frustrated with her efforts to avoid this conversation.

She pulled her scarf up, covering her ears. It was chilly outside. Autumn bid her farewell, it was now a beginning of icey grayness. One more peanut flew in the direction of a gray squirrel with a fluffy orange tail. It looked like he was trying to hit the animal now, not to feed it.

Any giggled, seeing how the scared squirrel jumped away from potential food.

"Few days ago I fainted in the office." He said distantly, with the freezing tone in his voice. "I didn't want to tell you, even asked Beth not to write anything about it in your diary. But apparently that's how it works in relationships. I can't ask you to share with me all your secrets and hide mine."

"Smart, very smart..." Any nodded couple of times. "Now that you opened up to me, I owe you an explanation..."

That was not a reaction he expected. Frustration increased in his face.

"Aren't you bothered with me being hospitalized?"

"You're sitting here now, so they did let you go."

"You're heartless, Gingerhead!" He exclaimed.

"At least one of us didn't overreact..."

"What do you know?"

"I know that Beth took it seriously..."

"She told you..."

"She kept her promise. She did not."

He turned to her all the way so fast that the bag fell on the ground, splashing peanuts all over the ground. Any was not looking at him, staring at her hands, rubbing the red spots appearing on her wrists from the cold. He was quiet. Asking was not an option. He knew that she would tell the story if he gave her enough time and space. She started already. Any took a deep breath and pulled her face deeper in a huge orange scarf. Probably she felt cold or just wanted to hide from her thoughts.

He looked at the pile of peanuts under the bench and mentioned with a sarcastic tone: "At least now I don't need to pretend that I enjoy feeding these stupid creatures."

121

"You didn't need to pretend."

"You wanted to feed them..."

"I want to do many things, it doesn't mean that you need to make all of them happen."

"Would you be happier if I told you that I'd rather spend some time indoors, not to freeze my ass on the park bench in the middle of winter."

"I would be."

"Weirdo."

"Liar!"

"What is boiling in your mind. Gingerhead? Spill it!"

Any looked at her hands again. It was obvious now that she had a massive internal struggle. He moved closer to her, hugging his way into an emotional conversation, taking her cold hands in his. Any didn't struggle, just put her head on his chest, still trying to find the way to hide from her thoughts. They spend like this few minutes, in the pure quietness of this ancient place.

"I felt that something was wrong that day. The moment Beth found out about you I just got this urge to have a look. She was so unbelievably emotional, I think she barely noticed me coming through. I bet she told you that she hardly remembered what she was doing."

"She did."

Any hid her face on his chest, digging under his coat.

"I couldn't resist and kept looking from time to time...even later, when you came over..."

Her quiet speech broke, voice cracked. He felt hot tears watering his shirt. He didn't say anything, just waited, looking at the mild sobbing movements of her head.

"You were convincing her not to tell me..."

"I was..."

"She agreed because there was something new to her in all of this, something she felt on her way to a hospital."

"What are you saying?"

"I blinked in your conversation for a split second. That was not something Beth would do, she would never tell anyone how she feels, apart from rare occasions of telling me. Next day was supposed to be mine, but I was so broken with all this that I just didn't see the light. This idea was going through my head over and over..."

"Light?" He used the opportunity to squeeze a question in between her sobbing.

She ignored it, saying: "This thought that if I don't show up, everyone's lives would be easier..."

Her tear flow increased, he put his palm on the back of her head, trying to calm her down, saying:

"You're an idiot, Gingerhead."

The way he said it, in his cold and distant manner forced her to put her face outside and look into his pale eyes. He was smiling with a corner of his lip. Same sarcastic evil smile she saw on his face the day they met.

"If you are not here, I have nothing else to live for." He said it emotionlessly. She felt his pain with every inch of her soul. It was enough to stop every doubt and heal every wound she had on her heart. She rubbed her eyes, removing the traces of tears and spreading her mascara under her eyes.

"Show off." She said, sobbing and smiling at the same time.

"Drama." He replied.

They were sitting like this for a moment, staring at each other. She was smiling, filling the space around with her external light. He was serious, with deep thoughts reflecting in his lifeless eyes.

"So will you tell me about The Light?"

"Nope." She said, trying to find a mirror in her bag, realizing how horrible she might look with her face swollen from tears and her mascara spread all over her face.

Any wiped the mirror with her palm and for a split second saw her reflection. It started blurring again so soon as the bathroom was steamy. Any took a towel from her head and wiped a mirror again with it. Her cheeks were hurting, probably burned with an icy cold wind. Her hair was peaceful as never before, just spread all over her shoulder. She smiled and looked around. Bathroom was bigger than her living room, covered with dark gray tiles, the floor was heated, and the light was very subtle. It definitely was a bachelors bathroom: no access hair products, no cabinets filled with something only females would need. There were only two things that were out of perfect design: an orange toothbrush in a dark gray cup and a towel in her hands. It looked like something she had never seen before, with autumn leaves embroidered all over it. Any looked at the mirror again. It was sweating, blurring her already not perfect vision.

She remembered how many years ago she was standing like this in her childhood home. It was different than, she didn't have anything, she didn't have anyone. Only Beth, the person whom she deeply loved and respected, but never met. She was

124

lonely, but was not trying to do anything about it. Being lonely was safe, being lonely didn't cause any trouble. It felt impossible to build a normal life, it still was, but it was different now. She was not a skinny teenager anymore. She was standing in a bathroom of a man, who made her his, who cared about her. She was almost sure that she was deeply in love now, but it was quite terrifying to admit to herself, making it complicated. It was easier to be lonely and to feel free, but she didn't want it anymore. She was still only one of two.

She smiled, remembering a poem she wrote as a teenager. It was still fresh in her mind, like the day she first wrote it down in their notebook. She pronounced the text now, the quietest she could, so he will not hear it:

"*Two souls in one body,*
Will never be able to meet.
Two girls in one life,
With a path full of limits and needs.
Two stories to tell,
Full of notes which will never be read.
Two pieces of puzzle,
With edges not meant to connect."

She remembered how Beth wrote under the poem with her neat cursive: "Maybe one day they will be ready to understand."

Beth was more a believer in humans when she was younger. She thought that if they played it right, they would not be locked in a mental health facility, they would be able to live a normal life without hiding.

Teenage Beth was naive, not like now. It took years for her to realize that hiding was not that bad, that hiding was an option, maybe the only option to avoid doctors and researchers. Any shook her head, trying to remove suddenly approaching teenage memories. She didn't want them now, she was happier than she had ever been and nothing was going to spoil it. Not today.

Her hair was drying now and its bright redness was not contrasting with the long black shirt she was wearing.

She put the towel back on the hanger and stepped in the bedroom, which was probably bigger than all her apartment. He was sitting in a huge bed with a book on his knees. Bright orange bracelet on his wrist was the only bright color in this room, full of high-tech design solutions. Bracelet and Any with her bright hair and volcanic eyes.

He looked at her, trying to read her thoughts, saying:

"You took your time."

"I just got lost in that huge room."

"Don't be jealous, Gingerhead. Your bathroom can barely fit two people, while one of them is standing in the shower."

"I'm not jealous of your cold gray apartment. At least mine is warm and cozy."

"You're talking about your apartment or clothes cabinet? I hate to disappoint you, but apart from your side, your apartment is filled with pretty much the same colors as mine."

Any rushed to him, jumping on a bed, landing on his knees, hurting him and herself, choking with laughter:

"That is why both of you need me in your lives!" She exclaimed.

Beth

Beth opened her eyes and stretched her hand in the direction of her phone immediately, looked at the screen and smiled. It was Monday.

It was a relief despite the fact that now she was in even bigger trouble. It didn't matter, not yet at least. Any was back. Any was here all day, Any definitely spent time outside. Beth looked at the irritated skin of her hands. That was something she would definitely avoid by simply wearing gloves, but not Any. Even this broken and cracking skin was a relief. Beth could forgive her other part anything now.

She pulled the phone closer to her eyes to be able to read notifications without putting glasses on. It was a lot. Karl, Les, clients. People were worried or just needed something from her. But only one actually surprised her. It was from her boss, it said:

"I'm in your living room, don't be afraid."

Sudden adrenaline rush ran through all her senses. Beth felt her skin numbing and heart pumping irrationally. She stood from the bed with the most dignity and calmness she could put on her face and opened the door.

He was there, sleeping, partly covered with the blanket, with a look of satisfaction and pease on his pale face. Beth stepped closer and looked at him with her eyes wide open, realizing that she never had a chance to do it before without feeling weird. His skin was so pale and contrasting with the black shirt that it looked unreal.

She coughed politely, thinking of how awkward it would be if he woke up now and saw her staring at him. He opened his eyes slowly and closed again, like what he saw was not a good enough reason to do it.

Beth coughed again, with more effort this time, saying:

"Can you please explain yourself?"

He answered with his eyes still closed:

"I'm happy that you saw the message before you came out."

"Me too..."

"Any didn't wanted to stay in my place overnight, so we came here."

"That explains why I am at home, but not you."

"I needed to talk to you."

Weird thought just appeared in his mind. Hours ago he was standing next to her bed, looking at sleepy Any, hiding her face in soft pillow, kissing her forehead good night. And now the person who looked exactly the same was not her. Beth still had Any's messy hair and colorful pajama on. But it was Beth.

He shook his head, not capable of comprehending it. Beth felt it and smiled ironically.

"Not her, right?"

"Just give me a moment." He whispered, closing his eyes, trying to switch, to convince his brain. Beth just stood on the same spot, patiently.

He opened his eyes again. Beth noticed something different now. His eyes were pale and cold again, he looked more absent.

"Interesting." She thought "He cannot be the same with both of us. He also switches."

"We got it sorted. Any is ok. I believe she just misread our communication on my hospital visit day."

Beth blinked slowly, understanding. Any got upset because of how close they were, she got jealous, she felt what Beth was feeling. That's what he was trying to say. She nodded silently, confirming that she understood. Her palms were sweating, she squeezed out with a shaky voice:

"I'm happy that she's back. I was worried."

He smiled. There was something new in Beth today, something he didn't notice before. She was softer, weaker if you can call it so. He knew that within hours she would gain herself back, become unbreakable again. Now he saw the cracks in her impeccable surface.

"Beth..." He said.

"Yes." She looked straight in his eyes and felt her cheeks blushing.

"I'm in love with her."

"She feels the same." She said uncomfortably, looking aside.

"Did she tell you?" He was surprised, Beth noticed his face firing up with pleasure.

"She didn't need to. We're not always separate, you know. Sometimes when one of us has strong feelings about something ... or someone... the other one feels it too."

Beth felt her cheeks burning. She literally just told him that she feels in love with him because she picked it up from Any.

This trait of their connection never worked well for her. One day she just woke up hating asparagus, which she was religiously eating and considering one of her favorites. Another day she casually craved that weird pop Any was drinking all the time.

But it was not about food or drinks anymore. Today she woke up feeling in love with the guy sitting in front of her on her couch.

Will it pass? Probably... She didn't know for sure, She was still hating asparagus though...

"What are you trying to say?" He interrupted her confused thoughts.

"Nothing more than I said already." Her guard was coming back now, volcanic cracks in her eyes completely gone.

"Why are you saying it?" Her cheeks were burning.

"Because we're busy destroying your life and it is normal to talk about it. Maybe it is still salvageable..."

"Maybe I don't need saving." Beth blurted it without thinking and realized how true it was. She just continued mumbling: "Maybe I don't need it to be saved, there is nothing to save..."

She suddenly felt so confused, took a few steps and dropped herself on the couch next to him. If he wouldn't move fast, she'd probably end up sitting on his ankle.

"We both know it is not true." He said, barely convincing. He was not actually sure if there was something worth saving in Beth's life. He knew only that she was a very dedicated hard worker.

"Do we?" Beth issued a sarcastic laugh.

"I'm not here to..." He couldn't finish.

"Why are you here?" Beth interrupted, without looking at him.

He sighed. For a moment he just looked at her, trying to read the cause of this struggle. It was like a system glitch. She reminded him of Any sitting on that park bench, trying to force feed stupid squirrels.

"To hear you out..."

It was sincere and sharp. Beth woke up from her dream and looked straight into gray eyes.

"You don't have many people in your life whom you can trust. Correct me if I'm wrong... I just want to give you an opportunity to spill it out. You can share with me. I'd rather die than betray you and you know it."

"Show off." She said through her teeth.

"At least you both finally have the same opinion about me." His lips bended in a smile and barely noticeable sparkle blinked in his lifeless eyes.

Beth stepped into the elevator, staring at her own reflection in a huge mirror. It felt weird. Since morning she had this feeling of her mind wandering, she felt not present in a moment fully, like her soul was randomly flying away and then coming back. She remembered everything that was happening, only this odd feeling... She looked at her reflection matching it with how she felt.

"What the hell is happening to me?" She mumbled.

Beth looked at her hands, like she needed confirmation that she still owes them and moved her fingers. Something was definitely off. Every once in a while since he finally left her apartment, she repeated the same actions.

"That's something new." Beth had blackouts before, when Any popped up, but it was not the same. She just felt like the anchor that was holding her in her body was weakened. She felt like a helium filled balloon, which was ready to fly away in the sky any minute if not the tiny strap that was holding it.

"Beth!" she heard once the elevator door opened.

"Les!" She tried to imitate the same tone.

Les was standing next to a gentleman, wearing a delivery uniform, holding a package in her hands. She looked as perfect as a woman can look. Her glossy blond locks spread all over her shoulders in a highly controlled way. Her high heels were the same color as her lipstick and her necktie. Dark gray suit matching her body so perfectly, like she had a personal tailor doing it overnight.

"I'm a bit busy now, but we need to catch up for coffee later." Les said with no sense of urgency. One of the things Beth admired in her was this sort of zen energy. Whatever happened, Les never looked stressed or overwhelmed. She would never lose it even if a deadly tsunami was heading her way with massive destruction. She always handled herself perfectly and Beth secretly admired her for this.

How badly Beth wanted to be like Les now, when ground felt like cracking under her feet.

"And Karl wants you." Les added with perfectly measured playfulness in her tone. Exactly enough to give Beth a slight hint that she suspected something going on between them.

She knocked in an opened glass door. Karl looked at her with no surprise in his eyes. He was expecting her.

They talked business for a while and then just stopped. Karl looked into her eyes with genuine concern.

"What's happening with you Beth?"

He saw the change, but he read it wrong. He thought it was about them, about their boss, about all this complicated work drama. In his eyes it was major, Beth was barely concerned about it now.

"Are we not seeing each other anymore?"

Seeing each other? That's how married men apparently put it. They were not dating... married men can't date, they were seeing someone. Beth felt slight frustration about it. She knew who she was and what they were doing, she agreed on being mistress willingly, so why was she annoyed?

For a fast moment her boss's face appeared in her mind. The way he treated Any... Not like she was number 1 or 2 in his life, but like she was the only woman on a planet, like she was the reason for his existence. Not in a maniac kind of way, he still played it very cool and distant, Beth just knew.

And here she was sitting in front of the man, in whose life she was woman number 2, maybe even 3. How did she allow this to happen?

"I don't want it anymore..." She said slowly and goosebumps rushed through her body like cold wind attacking bare skin. It felt right.

She smiled genuinely.

"It just doesn't feel right." This was the best reason she could find now and it was the correct one.

He nodded. He looked upset, but he held it together. He was not the man who would beg her to rethink or give him one more chance. He respected her decision and accepted it.

They are done now. Beth felt a relief, something shifted now and breathing was not that hard anymore. She walked out and on her way to her office she stopped and turned around.

"One more." She mumbled to herself.

She walked to her boss's office and knocked. He looked puzzled. Beth barely was initiating the meeting before, only in emergency situations.

"What happened?" He said with genuine concern. Beth dropped herself in a chair.

"I think I just broke up with Karl."

"Well... officially I didn't even know you're together." He smiled.

Beth smiled also. He made her feel comfortable. Like a friend, whom she could trust her secrets with. She didn't know when he became someone like this in her life.

"It may sound weirdly inappropriate today..." He paused, obviously looking for the right words. "Do you want to spend a day with me?"

Beth almost jumped in her chair. It felt like an alarm clock scaring you from a deep dream. She didn't see that coming. He saw the reaction and smiled with more evil in his pale eyes. That's exactly what he was expecting.

"Got you. I talked about it with Any and she sort of liked the idea of us getting to know each other." He added with a small coughing laugh: "You stuck with me now, you know."

He was right. He was part of their life and it would be easier if things worked out. Beth nodded. It felt weird and complicated.

"Stop thinking and planning, woman! Just let it go..." He said and added with noticeable persistence: "You take your bag now and we go to my car and go to any place in the world you want. Just don't look back and think about others, just for a change. Give me directions, that's the only thing I need."

Beth smiled. It felt so romantic and wild. It felt like something Any would do. Just chase something without any side thoughts, with no regret. One thought appeared in her mind and she couldn't hold it in, saying to him: "I'm not her, you know."

"I'm not asking you to be her..." He expected this hit from her side and reflected on it. "I'm asking you to be yourself..."

Beth looked at her fingertips again. Weird feeling of a helium balloon attacked her again.

"I feel weird today." She mumbled, still rubbing her fingertips.

He nodded, understanding it as a rejection of his offer.

"Is it anything I want?

Evil smile came back to his face. He whispered: "I'm rich."

"Show off!" She exclaimed and heard her heart pumping louder than ever. For a short second she lost it. The balloon stripe was broken and it flew away. Beth felt the floor moving under her feet, and someone switched off the light for some reason, or was it the sun that stopped shining?

She opened her eyes and heard machines beeping in the background. It definitely was blurry, she didn't feel glasses on her face. But she felt her hands and legs. Balloon was apparently tied back with the thickened stripe this time.

She was in a hospital bed, that was obvious. She reached to a bedside table, hoping that her glasses were there.

"Beth?" She heard from the corner.

It was actually a question. He was not sure which one of them was in front of him now.

"Yes..." She answered, clearing her throat, expecting him to be disappointed. But almost immediately she heard back: "Thanks God..."

He rushed to her bed not giving her eyes a chance to focus on his features. He got her glasses from somewhere and put them in her hand, probably understanding that she was barely differentiating his features from the background black and white photo of the mountain view.

Beth put her glasses on and was forced to close her eyes almost immediately, because everything immediately started to be so sharp and bright, a headache appeared in her temples.

She looked at him puzzled pronouncing her first thought aloud:

"Your hair looks longer."

It actually looked like he could pull it in a ponytail if he wanted.

"It grew..." He nodded.

"What happened?" Beth started feeling her heart pumping louder again.

"I wish I knew. Doctors looked kinda puzzled and I believe I heard something like: "It is impossible" a couple of times."

"How long..." Beth didn't finish the question, feeling her throat drying out. She coughed. He passed her a glass with the straw from the bedside table.

"Almost 2 months." He said with a tone of disbelief.

"Was I out all this time?" Beth felt her heart even louder.

"Yep... Both of you actually."

Beth hugged herself with her hands, she was shaking.

"2 months..." She echoed.

He nodded.

"You were here." She continued.

He nodded again and added "Most of the time... I wanted to be here when...something changes."

"I'm sorry." She whispered, feeling tears building up in her eyes.

"Don't be." He said firmly this time.

"What do the doctors know?"

"Apparently you had a unique condition which was not registered anywhere before. If you were not breathing and your heart wouldn't beat, they would consider you completely dead."

"What?" Beth couldn't hold sudden laughter. It sounded ridiculous.

"I know... You're getting more and more special every day." He smiled, for the first time since she opened her eyes. His eyes looked tired and even more colorless than before.

"You look tired." She said with a precise level of compassion, not to offend him.

"I just don't like hospitals."

"Me too. I guess no one does."

"Millions of hospital workers all over the world would not agree with that.... And you also looked quite comfortable here."

"I was... I guess." She nodded, observing her surroundings. She looked again at the bedside table and saw something she didn't notice before. Small bouquet of orange daisies.

Still looking at the flowers, Beth slowly pronounced: "When I woke up, you said my name, not Any's...

He also looked at the bouquet, picking the right words: "I wanted you to wake up first for some reason. It just made sense... and you're handling stress much better..."

He just kept mentioning all these reasons, but only one phrase was playing on repeat in her head: "Beth? Thank God..."

She tried to pull her knees closer and sit in bed and felt nagging pain in her muscles.

"Rusty..." she said with a short sarcastic laugh.

"Not like I'm complaining..." Beth said, putting an epic piece of omelet in her mouth. "But we're spending a lot of time together lately."

They were sitting in a diner with a beautiful city view from the window.

He nodded, looking at cars stopping on the signal and then taking off and disappearing from the view.

"We do."

It's been a month since doctors finally released Beth from the hospital. She was still taking time off from work, he insisted on that and she didn't resist. It was so weird to be out of the office for so long. She was wearing sweatpants now not only because they were comfy, but also because she got chubby now with this stress-free life and lots of delicious food.

"It may sound weird, but seeing you makes it easier..." He said quietly, still watching passing cars.

Beth nodded. She knew that she was not the one he wanted to see now, but it was close enough for him. She saw it on his face, which became more sad and pale each day. He was desperate, but trying not to show it to her.

"I wish I could..." Beth started, but was not able to finish the phrase as he interrupted her.

"I know you can't do anything about it."

Beth stared at her omelet for a second, thinking about pages of her notebook filled with letters to Any, begging her to come back first, asking if she was still there recently. She stopped writing a couple of days ago. She felt really crazy doing it now, without answers.

Sometimes she thought that maybe she was crazy after all and Any was only part of her imagination. That's what her parents thought. Imaginable friend of a little girl, who was having hard times finding friends. But there he was, sitting in front of her. The man, who was in love with another part of her, the man who believed that she was not imagining it. At least for now, he didn't give up believing. She wanted to tell him that Any will be back, she wanted to hold his hand tightly and look in the pale eyes, convincingly, but it felt wrong.

"You need to distract yourself." she said unexpectedly for both of them. "Go out of the country, switch off the phone, get disconnected and just...meditate, I don't know...do something that will put your mind somewhere else."

He looked at her and for the first time in days she saw a twinkle of the light in his eyes:

"That is not a horrible idea..." He said slowly.

"I was aiming at "good", but "not horrible" sounds encouraging enough."

"I was actually thinking about it." He said, looking at the moving traffic behind the window once again. "I just don't want to miss the moment..."

Beth bit her lower lip. Of course he didn't want to miss the moment when Any comes back. He spend two months in a hospital and now one more as her bodyguard just not to miss it. But there was only so much his exhausted mind could handle and it felt like it's going to crash soon.

Beth looked at her feet, she was wearing soft sock-like sneakers and her feet never felt that good. She was terrified thinking that soon she might need to give them up and squeeze her feet in high heels again. The only clothing she was still loyal to was the color. She didn't give up on dark and gray colors.

"You might be right..." He confirmed, distracting Beth from thoughts about her new sneakers. "I will go. For a week probably, just to restart myself." He looked at his reflection in a shiny tissue holder on a table and probably was not impressed with how tired he looked and how long his hair had grown. He looked completely lifeless next to Beth with her blushing cheeks and glowing eyes.

She nodded as there was nothing she could say. They both understood that it was needed, they both hoped that it would help.

Beth was sitting in a big armchair covered with a soft knitted blanket. She was holding a book in her hand. Someone knocked on the door and she stood up slowly, she knew who it was, she was expecting him. On her way to the door she looked at her reflection in the mirror. Her eyes were pale brown and her hair was gray now, only a few copper strands were there, reminding her how colorful her hair was once. Deep wrinkles were spread all over her face. Beth was old. She kept moving to the door slowly, probably scared to bump into something on the way. Her vision was barely a vision now, she was getting blinder each day. When she finally reached the door, she opened it straight, without checking who was behind it. She knew.

He was standing in front of her, barely recognizable. He looked as pale as man can be, his hair was short now, but the streaks of gray were very subtle. He was holding orange daisies in one hand and a bag with takeout food in another.

Beth smiled. It's been years. Didn't feel like it, but time definitely passed. This tradition was something they both followed religiously. He would come, they would talk for hours, he would leave and they would not see each other or talk for another year.

Every year Beth was terrified that he would not show up anymore, because it could mean only one thing.

She took flowers from him, putting them in a vase, which she had already prepared on a coffee table, next to a colorful orange knitted scarf and pile of photos.

"Still alive." He said.

"Same." She replied.

They smiled at each other with sadness in their eyes. Many years ago on this day Beth fainted in their old office and ended up in a hospital. But they were here on this day, not to remember this event. They were here because this was the day Any died.

Any

3...2...1...

She was sweating so badly that it felt like she woke up in a puddle. Her heart was pumping so badly and breathing was so heavy that it seemed like a mild panic attack.

"Oh, Lord." She said, touching her chest in desire to rip it open, so she will have more air in her lungs. She was awake now and the realization that it was only a dream was slowly settling in her mind.

Any felt how cool her wet sheets were and it felt even more unpleasant than her possible signs of heart attack.

It was not this kind of nightmare that scares you to death with the monsters or horrors. It was another type, but still. It felt terrifying.

Any looked at her hands. They were not looking old and soft anymore. The idea of this dream being a reality was slowly disappearing like a haze.

"Just a dream..." She mumbled, still not fully convinced as it felt so realistic.

Once her breathing went back to normal, she started noticing other things. Her body was sore. She remembered Beth complaining about it after Any performed an extremely long hike or something else, more physically exhausting that

Beth was used to. But Any never felt it before as Beth was not a fan of physical activities.

"That's new." She mentioned to herself, trying not to lose balance while taking glasses from the bedside table.

She noticed clothes folded there and a pair of comfy looking sneakers standing right where she normally put her feet on the floor while waking up.

"Interesting." She mumbled, not even planning to put shoes on and grabbing her notebook instead, waiting for the explanation.

The notebook felt heavier than before and was definitely fuller. Only a few pages were left blank now.

"What the..." Any started to say, realizing that almost half of it was filled with the neat cursive with the notes she didn't read.

The shock was building up while she realized that apart from being sore, her body felt heavier. She was chubby now. The feeling of being bigger than you used to was so weird. It obviously didn't happen overnight. Any knew that she was missing quite a lot.

She put the notebook aside, not having time to read it. There was something more urgent now. But with all the urgency she felt now, she was not able to move faster than her exhausted body was allowing to. Every inch of it was really sore.

"What was this workout, Beth?" Any breathed deep and kept moving until she reached the door of her closet.

"Yeah, now I get it..." She mumbled realizing why Beth was overdoing the physical activity. But that was not the thing she wanted now. Staring in this mirror gave her better understanding, but that was not what she needed.

She opened the closet and reached to her phone, laying on a shelf as usual. She never saw such an amount of message notifications before. Apparently what Beth was doing in their notebook, He was doing in a messages. Any didn't scroll through or read any of them. Just typed as soon as her sore fingers allowed. She was so worried at this point that tears were building up in her eyes.

"Hi." She typed, realizing how not enough it was considering circumstances.

It took a couple of exhausting moments until she saw the message back and she felt pain wired in every letter of this text:

"Gingerhead?"

She paused, feeling her tears sliding down her face.

"It's me. I'm here." She typed, understanding how ridiculous it might sound for a person who didn't know.

Few horribly long moments passed again.

"I'm on my way." He typed, probably from his car already. Any could imagine him actually dropping everything he was doing at the moment, no matter how important it was and rushing to her.

She looked at the mirror again. Apart from being heavier than she remembered, she noted looking healthier now, more lively. She looked like a person who actually enjoyed her life now, not like a person who barely had one.

He knocked. It made her heart beat faster again, not because she was nervous, but because it was oddly similar to what she just saw in that dream. She stood up and slowly moved to the door, just about the same as the old Beth did. There was only one difference now, Any was in charge now.

She opened the door and pulled the blanket back to her shoulder as it was sliding down now. He stood there and stared. For a short moment Any actually felt uncomfortable from this stare, like she didn't get it from him, but from the creepy stranger on the street. She pulled her blanket even more, trying to hide under it, to protect herself from this piercing look.

"Stop it." She mumbled, cringing from her own voice.

He did, slowly came inside and locked the door behind him. She never felt so short next to him. Even with her body feeling bigger now, she felt so tiny now.

"I'm sorry." He said and she realized that for him it also felt off.

"No flowers?" She smiled, realizing that she is still partly walking through the horror of her nightmare.

"I was rushing." He said, looking at his empty palms.

"Excuses..." She said making the best fake drama face she was able to.

"It is you..." He said it with such a sourness in his voice, that she actually felt how he was struggling to keep it together now.

"If it's not, it means that Beth is running the cruelest joke ever."

He passed her and dropped himself on a couch, rubbing his face with his hands, sort of trying to wake himself up just in case it was a dream... maybe one of many he had."

She moved closer, sitting next to him on the armrest, becoming almost higher than he was now. Any didn't know what to do or to say. This whole situation was so off already, but it could go sideways in any direction now.

She remembered her dream again. That's what he thought happened. He thought that she left him forever, he thought that she died.

"I have something to tell you." He said, looking straight into black eyes with volcanic orange cracks.

Milton Keynes UK
Ingram Content Group UK Ltd.
UKHW031825140224
437823UK00015B/339